CRYSTAL CLEAR

Cay David

KISMET™ is a trademark of Meteor Publishing Corporation

Copyright © 1991 Cindy Landon Lamar

Cover Art Copyright © 1991 Michaela Rangel

All Rights Reserved.

No part of this book may be reproduced or used in any form or by any means, by any means, without permission of the publisher. Any scanning, uploading, and distribution of this book via the Internet or via any other means without the permission of the publisher is illegal.

First Printing September 1991.

A KISMET™ Romance

METEOR PUBLISHING CORPORATION
Bensalem, Pennsylvania

Printed in the United States of America

CAY DAVID

Cay David has always loved reading, writing, and diamonds! Although her college degrees are in literature, computer science, and psychology, the gem trade fascinates her, and for years she has designed and sold fine jewelry. Despite her varied careers, however, writing is her true vocation. She shares her home in Texas with her husband of seventeen years and a cat named Leroy.

This book is dedicated to my parents, Bill and Dot
_____ who have always been there for me.

To my _____ Stan and Marilyn, and for _____
support and encouragement.

To my husband, Dave, for his incredible patience
and love.

ONE: DAVID

David has always loved his life, living within, and
_____
_____
_____
_____
_____
_____
_____

She wondered later if the shadow had been an omen, but by then it no longer mattered. He'd already ruined her life.

No, that morning all she'd been thinking about was paying the bills as she sat in her office. In the showroom below, bright sunlight streamed through the windows making it almost impossible for her to see. Suddenly, silently, ominously, the long, black Mercedes limousine glided to the curb and cut the glare. Immediately, the luxurious interior of Cummins Jewelry dimmed. The bells above the door chimed softly, and *he* walked in.

He turned and waved through the glass door at the chauffeur who had apparently been following him as he strolled down the street, a common way to browse on Rodeo Drive. The uniformed driver nodded once then rolled down his window, obviously happy to wait and watch the parade of haute-couture-clad women drifting by.

Chrystal felt her heart accelerate. Since she'd purchased Cummins from her brother two months ago, traffic in the store had been satisfactory, but she wanted—*needed*—more than that. Cummins had to be the most successful jewelry store in Los Angeles, and she was prepared to do whatever was necessary to reach that goal.

The customer walked slowly into the display area, casually unbuttoning the jacket of his Armani suit, looking comfortable, very comfortable, in the elegant shop. Through the two-way mirror in her office, Chrystal allowed herself the luxury of watching him without his knowledge, filling her eyes with his physical, almost overwhelming presence. Thirty feet of space and an inch of bulletproof glass separated them, but he still managed to project overpowering confidence and poise.

Fascinated, Chrystal watched him casually remove the wire frame glasses he wore, and she noticed for the first time that his dark hair was pulled back into a discreet ponytail. It wasn't very long, but long enough to say "Look at me." He dropped the glasses into his coat pocket, then with the grace of a large cat, he prowled to the first case, sliding a well-manicured hand over the glass.

Now thoroughly intrigued, Chrystal waited and watched. Normally, she might have been suspicious; jewelers were by nature. But something about this man, his posture, his aura of power, the quiet dignity, told her he wasn't a thief. She felt a tremor of foreboding, however, at his almost territorial pacing of her store.

She stood abruptly as if to dislodge her unease and tried to convince herself she was still worried about her bills, nothing more. Marching out the office door, she went down the stairs to the showroom.

Marion, her only sales clerk, a handsome black woman with long braids and startling almond-shaped eyes, nodded once.

"Good luck," she whispered then grinned as she brushed past Chrystal. "He looks like a live one."

Deliberately, Chrystal walked away from the man to the opposite side of the showroom and unlocked the display case, trying to look casual. Her father had been an aggressive salesman, practically attacking customers the minute they walked in the door. Chrystal's technique was exactly the opposite. She was always friendly but reserved, and timed her approach carefully, letting the client make the first move.

She pulled her favorite diamond necklace from the case to give her hands something to do while she studied the man further. He was taller than she'd first thought, and the perfectly tailored suit accentuated his wide shoulders and narrow hips. His face was interesting rather than handsome, with chiseled planes and straight angles, no curves to soften the harsh lines. The feeling of loosely tamed aggression and barely checked power was stronger close up, and she felt her pulse quicken as though she were preparing herself for a race.

A gold Rolex adorned his left wrist but the dial was plain, no diamonds. On the smallest finger of his right hand, he wore a polished gold ring set with a beautiful blue cabochon. She always wondered about men who wore pinkie rings; they weren't usually what they seemed.

His left hand was bare.

She used a time honored trick as he rounded the inside corner and came closer to the case where she stood. "That's a lovely piece of lapis you have there," she said with a smile, nodding toward his hand. "A stone of that quality is difficult to buy now."

He raised his eyes from the case he'd been studying and looked directly at her. For two seconds, she felt herself lost in the darkness of his look, as if she'd suddenly fallen into an unlit pool. Chrystal held his gaze and felt her mouth go dry, but she maintained her eye contact, believing it important in a sale.

He finally broke the connection and looked down at his own hand, the fingers splayed against the case. "Thank you," he said simply. "It was a gift."

I'll bet, Chrystal found herself thinking. *From some woman with full pockets and empty nights*. She blinked twice and wondered where that thought had come from.

"Why can't you get this quality anymore?" he asked.

She forced her attention back to the ring. "The best lapis comes from Afghanistan. Ever since the Soviet war there, it's been very difficult to get material out of the mines and to the markets. Most of the sites are very remote and even in the best of times, transporting the stones was an ordeal. Since the few roads they had were destroyed, it's almost impossible." She held her hand out to his. "May I?"

Expecting him to remove the ring and hand it to her, Chrystal extended her palm but instead of the ring, he put his warm fingers into hers and curled them tight around her hand.

She felt an instant shock, as though she were standing in a puddle of water and he was a bolt of lightning. His grip was strong, and his larger hand dwarfed hers. Unreasonable panic assailed her.

Her heart began to pound and her breathing turned

shallow. Lifting his hand closer, Chrystal pretended to study his ring while she gathered her wits. A crazy sense of trepidation swept over her while she tried to focus on the royal blue stone.

It *was* a very good lapis. Dark blue, almost violet, no white spots, only the desirable streaks of gold-like pyrite winking back at her. No dye, excellent polish, a good height to the cabochon itself.

"It's lovely," she repeated and dropped his hand.

He smiled as though he sensed her discomfort and was somehow pleased by it. "You're very knowledgeable. Are you the owner?"

"Yes, I am," she said and reluctantly held out her hand—again. "Chrystal Cummins."

"How do you do? I'm Maxwell Morris."

With as little fanfare as possible, Chrystal extracted her fingers from his. She'd had enough hand-holding for one day.

He glanced once more around the shop, looking at the elegant surroundings, then his eyes lingered on her. "I was under the impression an older man owned Cummins. You're certainly not old and definitely not a man."

She tried to tell herself he probably flattered every woman that crossed his path, but still, his expression sent her hand to her neck where she nervously fingered the pearls she wore. "You must be thinking of my father. He owned the store until his death about two years ago."

"And he left the business to you?"

"No, to my brother, but he tired of it, so I purchased the shop from him several months ago."

"I see. Well, you're clearly in charge then."

She wasn't sure what he meant, but her face was getting warmer, and changing the topic seemed like her only hope. "Are you looking for something special today, Mr. Morris?"

He smiled enigmatically. "I may be. Do you have anything unusual, out of the ordinary?"

A twinge of annoyance rippled down Chrystal's back. The man had looked in every case in the store; surely he knew by now that was her specialty. "All of my pieces are one-of-a-kind, Mr. Morris. I design them myself and do a lot of the setting, also." She answered his smile with one of her own. "Is this for you or a gift?"

He looked slightly off-kilter for the first time since entering the store. He'd obviously assumed she was going to ask him what he wanted to spend, she thought with a small touch of satisfaction.

"A gift," he said, then added, "for a woman."

Why am I not surprised? "Were you thinking of a bracelet or a ring—"

"Not a ring," he interrupted abruptly. He looked down at the pendant she held. "A necklace."

She followed his gaze to her hands. The heavy gold choker was the most expensive piece in the store; selling it would take care of more than a few of the bills waiting on her desk. She held the ornament up and tried not to look eager.

"This is certainly a lovely one. It's eighteen-karat gold, and the center stone is a five carat diamond." The yellow brilliance flickered in the bright lights of the store. "Actually, this is a canary diamond," she added proudly. "They're rather rare and very popular right now."

She swung the necklace into his open hand and waited for the inevitable. Anyone, even someone as apparently well-heeled as Maxwell Morris, would blink at the five-figure price tag.

The hand-knotted chain spilled from his fingers onto the black velvet pad resting on the counter top. In the mesh of gold, hundreds of tiny diamonds winked and sparkled, all highlighting the golden stone in the center.

"I waited a long time to find the perfect stone for that mounting," she said. "The piece took me over three years to design, and I only recently had the resources to complete it."

"I thought you said you'd just purchased the store."

For a second, Maxwell Morris's eyes took on a coldness that made Chrystal's delight waver, then just as quickly, he seemed friendly again. Could she have imagined the fleeting impression?

"That's true, but I've been designing jewelry all my life. I had this sketched out, then when I bought the store and the canary was in the vault, well," she shrugged her shoulders with a smile, "it seemed like fate. I had to carve the wax immediately."

"Obviously you know what you're doing. This is a gorgeous necklace." He looked down at the pendant then back up at her. "I'll take it."

To reconcile what he'd said with what she'd expected took several seconds. She prayed he didn't notice her hesitation as she fought to temper her excitement with skepticism. This was too easy. Maxwell Morris didn't look like the kind of man who would buy jewelry, or anything else for that matter, without knowing what he was getting.

She held out a jeweler's magnifying eyepiece. "Would you like to loupe the diamond first?"

His dark eyes captured hers and refused to let go. "I don't think that's necessary. You're a reputable jeweler, aren't you, Ms. Cummins?"

The challenge in his stare bothered her. "Of course," she said stiffly, "but it's good business to know exactly what you're buying."

"Do you always know?"

"I try, yes."

"Sometimes life deals us surprises."

"Then that's why you should look, isn't it?"

A gleam of concession flashed in his dark eyes before he shuttered them and spoke, taking the loupe from her hand. "You're absolutely correct."

He picked up the necklace, and she watched in amazement as he held the loupe to his right eye, brought the pendant closer with his left hand, then steadied his grip by placing his little finger on his right hand against the mounting. Most of Chrystal's customers didn't even know which side of the loupe to look through. He held the tools of her trade like a professional.

She felt her delight fade into apprehension. Maxwell Morris was not an ordinary customer. Could he be a spy from one of her competitors? Chrystal had heard of jewelers who sent scouts to other stores. She stared at him as he studied the choker carefully then handed the loupe back to her.

"Beautiful. The workmanship is superb, the design original, and the stone outstanding. I'll take it," he repeated.

Her pulse quickened and she beamed, mentally setting fire to the mound of bills on her desk. Smiling her thanks, she allowed her uneasiness to dissolve. "Would you like it wrapped?"

"Yes, please, if you don't mind."

Stepping to the desk behind the counter, Chrystal lovingly placed the piece in a gray velvet box and took one last look. The sparkling diamonds seemed to wink at her and say, "See how things work out? Why were you so worried?"

The delicately woven gold warmed under her fingers, and she felt a twinge of envy for the woman it was destined to adorn. Her gaze involuntarily went to the imposing man waiting patiently across the store. Was it for his wife? His mistress? Did he have one or the other? Or both?

Decisively, she closed the lid of the box. What ridiculously inappropriate thoughts! The *sale* was the important thing. Before she could think about it any more, Chrystal wrapped the box in golden tissue, tied a bow on top, and made out the receipt.

She walked back to the counter and handed them both to Maxwell Morris. From his inside coat pocket, he pulled out his wallet and a Mont Blanc pen, then filled out the blank check and handed it to her. "Would you like to call my bank?"

"I'm sure that's not necessary," she murmured. Los Angeles was, in a lot of ways, a small town. By the time he reached his limo, she'd know who Maxwell Morris really was.

Chrystal had the bank on the phone the minute the long Mercedes left the curb. Without bothering to look up his account, the banker confirmed Morris's draft, a great deal of respect apparent in her voice.

Marion filled Chrystal in on the rest, her black eyes snapping with interest. "He's a lawyer," she said and by the time the older woman finished her gossip, Chrystal knew Maxwell Morris's age (mid-forties), income (high six-figures), and preferences (young blondes). Was there anything left? Oh, yes, his client list was long and star-studded even though he'd only been in Los Angeles for four years. And yes, he was divorced, it'd been quite messy, scads of money involved.

That evening, in her small condo, Chrystal carried her lonely salad to the dining table, thoughts of Max still nagging her. Apparently the divorce hadn't taken all his money, but somehow the puzzling Mr. Morris didn't fit Chrystal's image of an attorney. The suit was definitely not Brooks Brothers and that hair—did he wear it pulled back in the courtroom, too? Only his voice seemed appropriate, low with liquid overtones. She could well imagine its persuasiveness, in the courtroom or the bedroom. Shivering, she moved to the open window, shutting it with a decisive push.

Chrystal turned back to the table and sat down, closing her mind, just as she'd slammed the window, to the dark eyes haunting her. She didn't have time to think idly about a one-time customer. A pile of paperwork waited, reminding her of more mundane things. "Bills, bills," she murmured, forcing her mind to the task. "Why couldn't Neal have been better organized?"

Even as she asked the question, she knew the answer. Her brother had never been responsible for anything more important than finding himself a good date on Friday night, and still her father had left him the store.

She concentrated on her other concerns, like how in the world could Neal get a bill from Howard Meyer for fifty carats of fine white melee and not be concerned? The shop used a lot of the smaller diamonds for repair work but fifty carats? She'd found nothing like that in the safe, and the books she examined so carefully before purchasing the store hadn't mentioned it. The notice must be a mistake.

As she stared at the pile of papers, however, her anxiety lessened. The sale she'd made today would more than cover the expenses she'd incurred since taking over the business. She wouldn't even have to dip into her savings.

Ignoring her dinner, she pulled Maxwell Morris's receipt from the stack and thoughtfully rubbed her finger over his sprawling signature, thinking of the beautiful pendant he'd purchased. Her first major sale, and it had to be the canary! The beautiful stone had come to symbolize everything she'd worked so hard for, and she'd already pledged to take the choker out of inventory and keep it for herself after Cummins got off the ground. Obviously, that wouldn't happen now.

What kind of woman would be receiving *her* necklace? Unlike herself, Chrystal was sure whoever she was, she would have no appreciation for the brilliance of the diamond or the preciseness of the cut. No, Chrystal mused, she was probably one of those California blondes who wore their men on their arms and their diamonds in their cleavage—and both would be pretty spectacular.

Maxwell Morris would want a woman like that, Chrystal thought as she tapped his check against the table. He'd need someone who could keep up with him and his flashy image. He'd drawn her attention too quickly, been a trifle too interested, as though he were trying to camouflage something. But things weren't always what they seemed in California, maybe she was mistaken.

She shook her head and pulled out her own checkbook, ready to pay her bills while she ate. Why did she care who he *really* was? He'd paid her debts and what else mattered? She'd never see the man again.

*　　*　　*

"He's baaaaaaaaack." Marion's drawn out voice
and tilted head drew Chrystal's gray eyes then sent
them to the two-way mirror above the desk. She'd
been sitting there gathering her thoughts to call Mr.
Meyer, and she hadn't even heard the bells signaling
the opened door downstairs. Instantly her heart thud-
ded as she recognized the well-dressed man.

A shiver of foreboding traveled down her spine.
There was nothing a jeweler hated more than seeing
a customer the day *after* a good sale, even if he was
as good-looking as Maxwell Morris.

Chrystal looked up at Marion. "Did he say what
he wants?"

The older woman shrugged. "Just that he wanted
to talk with Ms. Cummins."

Chrystal's eyes were drawn once more to the
glass. "Tell him I'll be right there."

Marion left to deliver the message, her braided
hair swinging with her steps. Chrystal watched her
speak briefly with the lawyer, and then he raised his
head and looked directly through the mirror and into
Chrystal's eyes. Of course, he didn't know he was
looking at her, she told herself sternly, so why did
she shiver?

He put a slim briefcase on the counter and folded
his hands over the top. He looked patient, self-con-
fident, and utterly at home, and even though Chrystal
knew his appearance meant trouble, she couldn't help
but appreciate the way he waited beside the glass-
topped case. The pose seemed oddly familiar, and
then she remembered with a start of what he
reminded her. The last time she'd visited the San
Diego zoo she'd seen a sleek black jaguar that wore

that same self-satisfied look. What had delighted her before now seemed suddenly sinister.

She instantly stood up and straightened her spine. This was her store, her turf, her business. If he had a problem with the necklace, she would kindly point out the signs posted around the showroom: Store credit only was issued on returns. No money back—this wasn't the Home Shoppers Network.

Downstairs, she held out her hand to Maxwell Morris and pasted a false smile on her lips. "Good morning, Mr. Morris. Was your gift a success?"

"I believe you could say that." He looked over her shoulder at the desk where Marion sat. "Do you have an office, Ms. Cummins, where we could talk a bit more privately?"

Chrystal felt her smile, fake as it was, slide slowly off her face. She swallowed hard. "Is there a problem?"

From his ears, he leisurely unhooked the curved wire frames of his glasses then removed a handkerchief from his inside pocket. He polished the lenses with slow, deliberate strokes. "That depends on you," he said conversationally.

The original stab of discomfort she'd felt at his arrival pierced her again, more sharply this time. This man was an attorney; he could make her life miserable if he desired. What on earth did he want with her? More importantly, why did she feel so threatened?

Chrystal made her voice strong. "I'm not sure I understand, Mr. Morris."

He looked up at her. Without the shield of the lenses, his gaze was even more penetrating. The shudder she'd been holding back rippled down her shoulders.

"Please," he said with a small smile, "call me Max. All my friends do."

She swallowed hard at his amicable voice. "Are we friends?"

"Not at the moment, but with time, yes, we will be."

"You seem awfully sure of yourself."

"That's one of the things I'm paid for, Ms Cummins—to be presumptuous."

His polished self-assurance made her own insecurity even more disturbing, and Chrystal tried to sound flippant to cover it up. "Well, then, I guess you earn your money well."

A brief shadow crossed his face, and he abruptly replaced his glasses on his nose and his handkerchief in his pocket. "Do you have an office?" he asked coldly.

She echoed his clipped voice. "Follow me."

As she opened the door to her cubbyhole, she inwardly cringed. She'd been too busy to make the office her own yet, and the crowded room still reflected Neal's lack of care. Maxwell Morris's office was probably paneled in ash, his desk a slab of marble, his couch a leather Roche-Bobois. She cleaned off the overstuffed recliner her father used to snooze in after lunch and said, "Have a seat."

She took the desk chair and swung it around to face Max. Their knees were practically touching, and in the close quarters, his aura of feline power almost overwhelmed her. Chrystal suddenly remembered the big cat in the zoo had been devouring a slab of something raw. She licked her dry lips.

Without a word, he looked out the window to the showroom below then glanced around the crowded office. She could well imagine what was going through his mind. Finally, he placed his briefcase on his knees and flipped open the locks. He removed a photograph and handed it to her. "Do you recognize that diamond?"

Her palms turned moist as she looked at the magnified image, blown up enough so that each facet was obvious. "Of course I do. That's the canary diamond I sold you yesterday." Her heart plummeted. "Why did you remove the stone from the setting?"

"I didn't. That photograph was taken before the diamond was set."

"I beg your pardon?" she said, genuinely mystified.

"You do acknowledge this is the gem you sold me yesterday?" he pressed.

With some exasperation, she nodded. "Yes, of course. You can see right here on the girdle," she pointed to the polished edge around the diamond, clearly visible in the photograph. "This diamond was gem-printed. A laser is used to burn an identification number on more important diamonds, almost like a brand, it's a way of—"

"I'm familiar with the technique, Ms. Cummins. Each number is unique so the diamonds may be tracked."

"Exactly." She put the photograph on the desk between them and dropped her hands into her lap. She didn't want him to see their trembling. "Does that bother you, Mr. Morris? You can't even see the number without a loupe."

"No, Ms. Cummins. It doesn't bother me that the stone was printed. What bothers me is that the stone was stolen."

TWO

"Stolen?" she repeated dumbly. "I don't understand, Mr. Morris. Are you saying—"

"I'm saying the stone belongs to someone else, Ms. Cummins, a firm which I represent. They hired me to find the diamond and return it to their stock. Needless to say, I was rather surprised when you sold the gem to me."

Chrystal's heart hammered with fright and uncertainty, but she ignored her anxiousness and turned it into righteous indignation.

"I think there's been a mistake here, Mr. Morris. That brilliant was in the vault when I bought this business. I'm sure if I were to look, I'd find a bonafide receipt for it. If your clients say the diamond was stolen, the theft must have occurred somewhere else down the line." She drew herself up, her spine an inch from the back of the chair. "We are not a pawn shop. We do not purchase goods off the street."

He smiled, and she suddenly felt like she was los-

23

ing ground. "Oh, absolutely, Ms. Cummins. I'm very aware of where you obtain your inventory. In fact, I represent several of the suppliers you use, in addition to the owner of this diamond." He brought a well-manicured hand to the knot in his tie. "They were all extremely gratified to know I'd found that particular stone, and they have great hopes that the rest of their inventory lies in your vaults."

Chrystal's heart began to pound in her ears and for a few moments, the image of Maxwell Morris, sitting in her father's old beat up chair, wavered. The polished steel of his glasses, the sharp lines of his suit, even the rock solid form of his body retreated to the background of her consciousness to be replaced with a voice from the past. "Women don't know how to run a business," her father's ghost boomed at her. "They're too flighty to control inventory, can't keep track of the bills."

She blinked and refocused on the smug lawyer's face. "I have no earthly idea what you're talking about, Mr. Morris. Before I purchased Cummins from my brother, I examined the books very carefully. There were no outstanding debts in his records."

"Did you check the inventory?"

A small flame of anger flickered as he echoed her father's fictitious words. "Of course, I checked the inventory."

"Against the books?"

She gritted her teeth. "Yes."

"And they jived?"

"Of course, they *matched*," she said coldly. "I wouldn't be much of a business person if I didn't examine the books before buying a business."

His voice turned blunt. "Then your brother cheated you, Ms. Cummins. This company owns none of the inventory in those vaults or in the cases in your showroom." His eyes were chips of ebony. "You've got a very big problem on your hands."

Chrystal felt as though the smooth-talking attorney had hit her in the stomach. Her back slumped into the contour of her chair, and as she felt herself go faint, she closed her eyes.

Instantly, he put his briefcase on the floor by his feet and reached out to touch her arm. "Are you all right?"

Her eyelashes fluttered open. "Oh sure, I'm fine," she said. "Just a little warm, that's all."

His forehead wrinkled with concern. "Can I get you a glass of water or some coffee? Anything?"

"No," she whispered.

But he'd already disappeared down the steps to the water cooler. She heard him run back up the stairs, then he thrust a paper cup into her freezing palms. "Drink it," he ordered.

She brought the cup to her lips, but before it got there her hand trembled violently. Mortification flamed her face as the cold water splashed over her blue silk dress, and she felt herself go numb. This was no way to act during a business crisis!

Immediately he pulled out his handkerchief and began to pat the fragile fabric, but the water seemed to spread even more. He raised his eyes to hers.

Huge tears ran down her ivory cheeks and plopped down into her lap. She'd been so cool, so restrained, so private, he couldn't believe she was actually crying. Her embarrassment was almost painful to see. He couldn't tell what bothered her more; his bad news or her lapse in control.

Max was already out of his chair and on his way to put his arms around her when he realized that would only would add to her humiliation. He stopped in mid-flight.

"I'm sorry," he murmured automatically, "I didn't know, I thought your brother and you, well, I—"

For a single heartbeat, he stared into Chrystal's clear gray eyes. If Max had ever thought she'd been working with her brother to cheat his clients, that misconception disappeared. Nothing but grief filled their translucent depths. Feeling oddly relieved, he slid back into his own seat.

From the moment he'd stepped into her shop until now he'd felt like a tightrope walker. His first loyalty was to his clients, but how could any sane man avoid the peril of those enormous, silvery eyes? Their calm and peaceful serenity beckoned to him like an oasis in a desert, and he knew with little persuasion he could fall into their depths, never to come out.

She swiveled to her left and plucked a tissue from a box on the corner of the desk. Turning her head, she quickly patted her cheeks then faced him once more. "I'm sorry," she apologized stiffly, "but I'm sure you understand that this is somewhat of a surprise."

"It always is," he said, hating the cynicism in his voice. "Nine times out of ten, the disputes I handle are family ones." He bent down to his briefcase and removed more papers. "The claims I've received against your business are extensive, but the owner of the canary stone holds the largest claim, so far."

"So far?" she repeated faintly.

He didn't think her ivory skin could go any paler; it was almost transparent now. In fact, he could see her pulse pounding at her temples, and the sight affected him strangely as if he'd just spied something private and intimate. He cleared his throat uncomfortably; never before had he experienced twinges of sympathy for a client on the opposite side of the table.

"Yes, so far," he finally answered. "Usually when cases like this break and become public, claimants come out of the woodwork. Because you operate in such a tight-knit community, I'm anticipating the news to travel fast."

"Then your case will be even stronger," she said bitterly. "I don't stand a chance, do I?"

"I wouldn't say that—"

"But you'd bet on it."

"Let's just say you are in trouble. But if you cooperate, I'm sure we can—"

A discreet knock on the door of the office interrupted. "Yes?" Chrystal answered.

Marion opened the door. "I'm sorry, but Mr. Meyer is downstairs. He insisted that I come get you."

Chrystal nodded once. "Tell him I'll be right there."

Her eyes returned to Max, and she licked her lips. "Would you excuse me just a moment?"

"Of course," he answered. "Take your time. I'll wait."

The flicker of loathing that crossed her face told him she'd be happier if he left and never returned.

She grabbed another tissue off her desk, made a quick swipe across her eyes, and opened the door. A few seconds later, he watched her enter the showroom, as cool and collected as when he'd first come through those doors.

"Hello, Mr. Meyer. It's so nice to see you again." Her calm voice came into the office, and

Max smiled with reluctant respect. Now he understood the murmurs he'd heard earlier when Marion
had been speaking downstairs. Not only had Chrystal
installed a two-way mirror but microphones in the
showroom, as well. He raised his eyebrows. This
lady was prepared for business.

"How is your wife these days? I haven't seen her
in a long time," Chrystal continued to chat up the
slight man in front of the counter. He looked like a
bum, but Max knew better. People in the jewelry
trade often dressed that way while in their pockets
they carried thousands of dollars' worth of what they
called "goods."

"She's still putting up with me, I can't complain." Mr. Meyer smiled apologetically then looked
around. "A nice place you've got here, Chrystal,
very nice. Your father would approve."

Max watched her spine straighten. Did she always
do that when she felt threatened?

"I doubt that, Mr. Meyer, but we'll never know,
will we?" She abruptly switched tone. "I'm glad
you came by. I know there's a slight problem . . ."

"Slight?" The older man's voice rose. "Slight?
You call fifty carats of melee slight? I know you
young people have different values, but fifty carats
of fine white goods is not what I'd call slight."

She reached across the counter and touched his
sleeve. "I wasn't trying to indicate that, Mr. Meyer.
It was a manner of speaking, I meant—"

"Don't matter, girlie," he suddenly growled. Max
was shocked at the transformation. A few seconds
earlier the old man had been talking like a loving
uncle to a favorite niece.

"You own the store now. Your brother bought
those goods, and you have them, I don't. So you

pay me, right? It's simple." He waited expectantly, his hands fumbling in his pockets.

Chrystal's expression grew chilly. "Mr. Meyer, when I purchased the store, I examined the books and the inventory. There was no bill for your melee then and no small stones in the safe, and I *know* I haven't purchased anything like that from you." Her voice took on a desperate tone Max hated to hear. "Are you sure Neal bought those diamonds from you? He didn't have them on memo, did he?"

"For ten months? Memo?" He raised one gnarled hand and flicked his wrist. "Forget it, sweetie. I don't loan nothing for ten months. He bought 'em. I billed 'em."

Max felt his hackles rise. What right did this man have to harass her? She might owe him money, but that didn't justify this kind of attitude. The sense of fairness that turned him to the law in the first place forced him to his feet.

Chrystal stood helpless in front of the onslaught. The old man continued. "I ain't leaving till I'm paid, sweetie. Go get your checkbook."

The bells over the door jingled softly and all eyes went to the front. Two well-dressed women entered, their furs sleek and expensive, their makeup perfectly intact. Max watched Chrystal turn to Marion. With a flick of her eyes, she sent the black woman to the waiting women.

Chrystal dropped her voice, and Max leaned forward, as if he could hear better. "Mr. Meyer, if this business owes you money, then you *will* be paid, I promise you, but I can't right now. I've got some trouble—"

"Trouble?" he repeated in a loud voice. "You're

just imagining trouble, honey, you ain't seen nothing yet.''

The two women glanced up from the case where they'd been examining earrings and lifted their perfectly feathered eyebrows at each other. Max had been married to a woman just like that, and after years of practice, he knew exactly what that look meant.

"Look here, sweetheart, it ain't personal—''

"Mr. Meyer, could you please lower your—''

Max didn't wait to hear the old man's answer. He opened the office door and hurried down the steps. In two quick strides he was by Chrystal's side and extending his hand. "How do you do? I'm Max Morris, Chrystal's attorney.''

The old man's eyes opened wide, and his mouth snapped shut. Chrystal stood by silently, her huge eyes darting between Max, Meyer, and the two women at the end of the counter. "Is there some problem?'' Max said easily.

"Not as long as she pays me what she owes me.''

"Then there's no problem,'' Max said with a deceptive smile. "Give me your bill. I'll see that it's taken care of immediately.''

Meyer fished around in his voluminous pockets, while Chrystal stared strangely at Max. She hadn't uttered one word since he'd come downstairs. Her dark hair framed her pale face, and he forced himself to quell the sudden urge he had to smooth her bangs.

"It ain't here. I had it just before I left, now I can't find it,'' he mumbled.

"Fine,'' Max replied. "Drop the bill in the mail when you locate it. I'll see to it.''

He drilled the shorter man with a penetrating look, challenging him to say more, but Meyer disappointed him. He nodded once then shuffled out. Max felt his earlier surge of adrenalin fade, just like it did after a verdict was read. In the end, someone always lost. He turned to Chrystal.

"Are you all right?"

"Thanks." Her eyes said more than the one word she uttered.

Her gratitude chilled him; he'd said once before he never wanted to see that look in a client's eyes, and that's when he'd left his public defender position. "Forget it," he said brusquely. "Look, I've got to go. I have to be in court in an hour. I'll come back tomorrow, and we can talk some more."

"You don't think I'm going to skip town now that I know what's going on?"

He looked at her sharply; apparently the appreciation had turned to apprehension. "I'm not worried. If you do, I'll find you."

Marion's eyes grew round and large, her broad forehead wrinkling. "But, Chrystal, how could Neal have done this? Wouldn't I have known?"

They were closing the shop, and this was the first opportunity Chrystal had found to tell Marion Max's news. She shook her head, dismay deepening her voice. "How could you have known, Marion? I didn't, and I examined those accounts inside and out before I paid him for the store." Her eyes threatened to fill, but she held her tears in check. "Neal's done some pretty bad things, but this—this is really hard to take."

Marion shook her head in disgust. "Your own brother, I can't believe it. Well, on second thought, maybe I can." She sighed deeply. "Those sales today help?"

With a sinking heart, Chrystal bleakly shook her head. "Not enough. We're talking big bills." With a horrified gasp, Chrystal had a new thought.

"Marion, do you think Max could jail me? Is this a criminal offense?" Suddenly, visions of bare cell walls and cold iron bars came into her mind.

"Oh, honey, I don't think so. He wouldn't have left like he did if it was that bad." Marion patted her shoulder, her tall girth reassuring. "What are you going to do? Get a lawyer of your own?"

"I don't know. It sounds like I don't have enough money to go grocery shopping, much less lawyer shopping."

"You don't have to have money to get a lawyer, honey. I had a neighbor whose landlord wouldn't return her rent deposit, said her cat peed on the carpet. He was going to charge her fifteen hundred dollars just for that. She went down to that free legal clinic, and one of those young hot-shot attorneys helped her right out, didn't charge a dime."

Chrystal smiled weakly. "I don't know, Marion, but this looks a little more complex."

"Well, try not to worry, you'll manage, baby. Just like your father always did."

"Dad never had problems like this."

"Well, that's true, but he always had aggravations of some sort. No business operates smoothly all the time."

"Yes, but this isn't exactly a small glitch, Marion." She forced the panic from her face. "I'm responsible for all the debts Neal managed to accumulate operating this business. I bought it lock, stock, and barrel."

The dark-skinned woman put the last case into the

vault as Chrystal spoke, then she stepped back and slammed the door shut. "Yeah, well, you're a helluva lot smarter than your brother, too. With your chutzpa, not to mention those gorgeous looks, you'll do fine. Don't worry, it'll work out."

Chrystal locked the door behind the saleswoman then cut off the overhead lights and leaned against the nearest counter. She had serious doubts this would "work out." Finally alone, she allowed the tears to flow as she stared at the barren glass cabinets, their velvet trays bare and waiting. If she couldn't figure out a way to overcome Neal's debts, she was going to be looking at empty cases for a long time.

The next morning, Chrystal's nerve endings seemed to be connected to the bells above the door; every time someone entered the shop, she'd jump, and by mid-afternoon, she wanted to scream. Why hadn't Max returned?

Five minutes before she was going to lock the door, the bells tinkled softly. Chrystal raised panic-filled eyes then felt her disappointment surge and drain. It wasn't Max, but at least it was a customer who would divert her.

"Mrs. Meriweather, how nice to see you," Chrystal exclaimed. A genuine thread of welcome ran through her voice. The first time the society woman had entered the store, Chrystal had been terribly intimidated by her reputation and demeanor, but now they were fast friends. Like a majestic ship, the gray-haired matron sailed into the showroom, diminishing its size by at least half. Resembling nothing so much as a miniature dinghy, a tiny rat terrier on a slim gold leash scurried along beside her, his diminutive legs pumping to keep up.

"Hello, my dear," she boomed. Her teased and coiffed hair moved up and down as she took in every detail of Chrystal's appearance. "Chrystal," she scolded gently, "you look a little peaked, I must say. Are you working too hard?"

Chrystal smiled and hoped the dark shadows under her eyes would disappear. "No, Mrs. Meriweather, just busy, I guess." She looked down at the little dog. "And how is Little Bit today?"

At the sound of his ridiculous name, the pooch looked up with reproachful eyes. The appellation clearly upset his dignified bearing, but he suffered in silence. Mrs. Meriweather gave a tug on the leash, and he reluctantly scrambled closer, anxious to avoid the pull.

"Isn't my little sweetheart gorgeous?" she cooed, and the dog's eyes rolled backwards. Chrystal couldn't tell if it was from the tight leash or embarrassment. "Do you see what he's wearing today?" the stout woman asked coyly.

Chrystal bent over the case to get a better look then gasped. "Mrs. Meriweather, that's your gold bracelet! What is it doing around that dog's neck?"

"Doesn't it look precious on my baby?" she beamed. "Nothing's too good for my Little Bit, is it, sweetum?" The dog endured a few moments of petting then started to growl. Mrs. Meriweather stood up abruptly, switching gears with her usual aplomb. "I need something for that worthless daughter-in-law of mine, Chrystal," she announced in an imperious voice. "She's going to have a birthday, and I want to give her something big enough to shut her up for once."

Chrystal swallowed her smile. "Did you have something special in mind?"

"No, only it has to be spectacularly expensive, or she won't be sufficiently impressed. What do you recommend?"

Chrystal sat the woman down and began to empty her cases. An hour later, nothing had been selected, and nothing remained to be shown.

"I'm sorry, Mrs. Meriweather, but that's all I've got at the moment." *And all I'll probably have for quite some time,* she thought desperately. She searched her brain feverishly. "Exactly when is her birthday?"

"Next month, May 15th."

"Then her birthstone would be an emerald. Does she have any?"

"Heavens no, darling. Now she's positively salivating over my jewels. If I don't buy her some soon, she'll knock me off to get mine! The woman was penniless before she snagged Arthur Two."

Mrs. Meriweather's booming laughter filled the showroom, and Chrystal had to grin. Her late husband had been "Arthur One," therefore their son was "Arthur Two." The name always made Chrystal think of airplanes instead of people.

Suddenly Chrystal had an inspiration, but just as she began to speak, the door opened, and the man she'd been waiting for all day strolled in as if he owned the place. Behind Maxwell Morris trailed an older man with a large cigar.

Chrystal caught her breath while nervous hands automatically smoothed her hair. She prayed Max wouldn't say anything in front of Mrs. Meriweather. Chrystal liked the eccentric matron, but her reputation for gossip was renown.

"I'll be right with you," she said politely to Max then returned to Mrs. Meriweather, suddenly anxious to get her out of the store.

But the older woman's eyes had already left the sparkling case before her and turned to Max. "My God, you naughty boy," she cried. "Where on earth have you been? I haven't seen you since Arthur One died."

Chrystal's dread increased. They knew each other? The matron stood, abruptly pulling Little Bit off the floor two feet as she enveloped Max in a hug and a cloud of "Joy."

Max's eyes met Chrystal's over the helmet of gray hair, and he smiled apologetically as though the woman's enthusiasm was somehow his fault.

"Elizabeth, how nice to see you again," he said in liquid tones, extracting himself gracefully and bringing her hand to his lips. "You aren't in here picking out an engagement ring, are you, Elizabeth? You promised you'd wait for me."

Gales of giggles racked her sturdy body, and a pale blush covered her powdered cheeks. Chrystal felt the urge to roll her eyes back as far as Little Bit had earlier.

"Oh, aren't you a cad!" Mrs. Meriweather cried. She playfully punched his arm. Chrystal had to smother a giggle herself as he stepped off-balance. "No, no, I'm buying a bauble for Claudia," she turned and frowned, "or rather I'm trying to."

Chrystal interrupted smoothly, trying to regain some form of control. "Why don't you give me two weeks, Mrs. Meriweather? One of my dealers is in Zambia now, and I know he's bringing back some lovely stones. Let me call you then."

To Chrystal's immense relief, Mrs. Meriweather

beamed. "Excellent, an excellent idea, my dear."
She bussed Max thoroughly, sniffed at the other man
as though his presence offended her, and yanked on
Little Bit's chain. "Come along, darling, come
along."

Chrystal breathed a premature sigh of relief just as
the woman reached the door and turned. If she'd had
a fan, Chrystal was sure Mrs. Meriweather would
have fluttered it.

"Maxwell, *you* aren't planning on getting married
now, are you? It'd break a thousand hearts if you
were here buying some lucky girl a diamond."

Max's eyes met Chrystal's, and she held her
breath, waiting for his answer. Her reputation was at
stake, and knowing the real reason for his presence
made Chrystal wish the floor would open up and
swallow her, but the marble tiles refused to crack.
She tolerated his dark gaze and lifted her lips in a
tight smile.

He finally looked over at the waiting woman and
grinned. "I can't tell you that, Mrs. Meriweather.
Why would we want to cause all that pain and suffer-
ing? Besides, it might not work out, then where
would I be? My harem might get low."

The flood of relief Chrystal felt couldn't wash
away her irritation. Why should she be grateful that
Max didn't tell Mrs. Meriweather he was about to
ruin her business? Suddenly, his poise and smoothness
grated on Chrystal's raw nerves like sandpaper, and
she had an overwhelming urge to let him know
exactly how she felt.

But she didn't.

As usual, she hid behind the cool façade she'd
developed as a child, and let their silly banter continue until Mrs. Meriweather finally satisfied herself

and left. As soon as the door closed, Chrystal turned to Max. Despite her anger, she wanted to throw herself at his feet and plead for mercy.

But she didn't.

"How are you today, Mr. Morris?" she said politely.

"I thought we agreed on Max."

She smiled her acknowledgment then turned to his companion. She'd watched him since he'd entered the store, and she didn't like the predatory prowl that had taken him up and down her cases. He made her nervous. If he hadn't come with Max, she probably would have already called her security service, just to be on the safe side.

He finally stopped his pacing directly in front of Chrystal and Max. The extra fifty pounds hanging over his alligator belt jiggled as he reached inside his coat pocket and removed a gold lighter. "Big H" was spelled out in diamonds across the top. His nails were polished, and his hair hung over the turned-up collar of his white silk suit. He looked like he'd just stepped off a plane from Las Vegas.

Max broke in gruffly. "This is Hiram Plotsky, Chrystal. He's the owner of the canary diamond."

She dropped the hand she'd extended as her proprietary feelings exploded. Now she understood why he'd been examining her cases so intently. He was seeing if there were any other stones he could claim as his!

Like a mother cat with kittens, Chrystal gathered up the pieces she'd been showing to Mrs. Meriweather and put them on the shelf behind her, out of sight.

With her back turned to the two men, she strug-

gled to contain her indignation, but she fought a los-
ing battle. Hiram Plotsky didn't own this store; she
did, and it'd be a cold day in hell before he got his
fat, cigar-stained fingers on any of her pieces.

THREE

Max got one good look at Chrystal's expression before she managed to turn. Instantly, he regretted bringing Hiram. He glared at the large man beside him. Hiram Plotsky was not one of Max's favorite clients, however he was one of his more reliable ones. Someone was always suing Hiram and vice-versa, probably because of Hiram's stellar personality.

"Why didn't you shake her hand?" Max whispered. "For God's sake, Hiram, a little courtesy wouldn't kill you."

Small, piggish eyes regarded Max with disbelief. "Courtesy, smourtsey! Why should I be nice to her? That's my stone, and I'll be damned if—"

"Shutup, Hiram, she's coming back."

Max removed his glasses then smiled as Chrystal came around the case. "We'd like to talk to you about the diamond, Chrystal. I've got a proposition for you that might solve everyone's problems."

Her cold gray eyes told him she seriously doubted his claim, but she was too much of a lady to voice her opinion. Today she wore a pale pink Chanel suit that emphasized her black hair and porcelain skin, and the way she looked made Max wish he could tell her their presence was a big mistake, but he couldn't. Instead, he smiled again and nodded toward her office. "Shall we?"

She pursed her lips tightly and nodded once then led the small procession to the back of the shop and up the stairs to her office. For a few awkward seconds, Max thought Hiram wouldn't be able to squeeze into the tiny room, but he finally managed to slip into the chair opposite Chrystal's desk, while Max took the one closer to the door. With three people, the space seemed even smaller than it had the day before.

Hiram nodded toward the showroom. "Nice place you got here."

"Thank you," she said stiffly. "You have quite an establishment yourself, Mr. Plotsky."

Max could tell exactly what she thought of it, too. Hiram's retail store, a ten thousand square foot showroom which sat on a highly visible corner of Beverly Center, featured rock music and saleswomen who looked like extras from Universal Studios.

Hiram blew a haze of smoke into the tiny office. "Yeah, well, like I always say, 'It's a real gem.' " His laugh trailed off into a cough, then he continued. "I was the first jeweler in LA to offer free limos to the church for any bride who bought a stone over three carats. Pretty good, huh?"

"I suppose so," Chrystal answered, "but I have to admit, I've always wondered about that." She paused slightly as though considering the idea. "Do people who can afford that kind of stone really want a ride to the church in a car with 'Hiram's Hot Rocks' written on the side of the door?''

Max closed his eyes and ducked his head into his open briefcase, trying to hide his grin. He'd been worried about Chrystal? He should be more concerned with Hiram's welfare.

Before Hiram could reply, Max snapped his case shut and cleared his throat, anxious to get started. "Chrystal, Hiram and I realized that you didn't know the stone in question belonged to him. However, that does not negate the fact that it *is* his diamond. Now there are a couple of courses open here. I've gone over the options with Hiram, and he agrees that because of your location, my suggestion is the best.'' Max raised his eyes from the papers he held. "Hiram would like to buy you out.''

Chrystal stared at him as if he'd suddenly grown horns, and he felt a moment of irritation when she didn't reply. "This is a very generous offer, Chrystal.''

"Excuse me if I don't quite see that at the moment,'' she replied. A flash of uncertainty crossed her face so quickly that Max wasn't sure he'd even seen it. "Can't I just return the stone to him?'' she asked in a more subdued voice.

Max tried to soften his answer with a courteous voice, but nothing could change the meaning of his words. "I'm afraid not, Chrystal. You see, Hiram has lost potential income because you've had the stone. Now, you owe him more than the diamond's worth, not to mention the check I gave you for it. I'll need that back, then—'' He stopped at her stricken expression.

"I, I spent that already. I paid off some other bills with it.''

He'd hoped she wouldn't say that, but had sus-pected she would. He nodded his head. "We'll have to add that amount to the payoff," he said gently then, loathe to continue, went on. She had to know it all. "Unfortunately, there are all the other suppli-ers with claims, too. Hiram's offer would allow you to pay them off."

She nodded mutely, her gray eyes reminding him of twin silver lakes he'd once seen in Sierra Nevada in the dead of winter. Max cleared his throat and continued. "Not only is Hiram ready to drop the charges, he's allowing you to bow out gracefully, your credit intact. You would be free to open another store in a different location. A fresh start."

"I don't want a fresh start," she said suddenly, waving a hand at the small office and the showroom beyond. "This has been my family's store for over twenty years. If I moved, I'd lose more than just my location. I've got tradition here, the Rodeo Drive association, my good name."

"Yeah, and that name ain't gonna be worth squat soon," Hiram broke in. "When you go down, you're gonna go big. There ain't a supplier in town that'll touch you if you don't pay them bills, and soon, too."

"I have every intention of paying back every dime my brother owed, Mr. Plotsky. If those bills are legitimate, I'll pay them. You can bet *your* reputation on that."

The color rose in her cheeks, and Max leaned back in his chair, surprised at her reaction. From the little he'd found out before taking on the case, he'd thought Chrystal Cummins would have been delight-ed with the offer. She had no experience in business, little capital, and no backing.

Hiram stuck his cigar firmly into the corner of his mouth and spoke angrily around it. "My reputation ain't got nothing to do with this, sweetheart. I'm trying to do you a favor, and you're acting like I just pinched your butt."

Chrystal's eyes turned pale gray, and her back stiffened. Her voice was soft and refined when she spoke. "As far as I'm concerned, Mr. Plotsky, you can take your offer and cram it up your own—"

"Whoa now, let's all calm down," Max interrupted smoothly, trying to hide his surprise. She had a lot more spunk than he'd originally thought. "As I said when I began, there are a couple of alternatives, and I've only mentioned one. Let me outline the other, Chrystal. Perhaps we can find a compromise that we all can live with."

Those gray eyes turned on him, and Max felt an icy blast of scorn. The disadvantage he'd imagined her to be under suddenly seemed insignificant in the face of her determination. He continued, feeling more and more uncomfortable. "You owe a lot of people a lot of money, Chrystal, and most of them contacted me since they knew Hiram is my client. If you want to work this out and keep your business, we might be able to consolidate their claims and develop a payoff schedule that would keep the problem out of the court system. Hiram would be the largest creditor, of course, and should you fail to pay, he would take the store."

"And if I fight you?"

He took off his glasses and looked at her over his briefcase. "Naturally, that is your option, if you desire. I can recommend several good attorneys, an excellent clinic in fact, but," he lowered his voice into persuasive tones, "believe me, Chrystal, this would be the easiest way out."

Her back stayed ramrod straight. "What makes you think I want the easy way out, Mr. Morris? I've never taken that route before. Why should I do that now?"

If she'd said anything else, he might not have understood, but with those few words, Chrystal's ambitions became clear to Max. Suddenly, he realized: They weren't just threatening her business; they were taking on her dreams, and it'd take more than a few bills to destroy that aspiration. His admiration, and his dilemma, grew.

"We want to help you, Chrystal. We can all work on the same side, for the same goal, if you'll let us."

Her laugh was bitter. "Maybe we should define that goal, Mr. Morris. Mine is to keep my store. Is that your goal, also?"

"Yes," he said instantly, pressing on his advantage of his new understanding, "because my primary objective is getting my clients their money. If we shut you down, you have no way of paying them back. Frankly, we could file charges and put you in jail, but that's just not the way I operate."

For a moment, she looked as though she'd like to believe him, then her expression grew cold again. "Do you have any more options, Mr. Morris?"

He shook his head. "Not really. Of course, if you could simply pay my clients what you owe them . . ."

"At the moment, that would be impossible. I depleted my resources when I bought the store from my brother. If the rest of the bills rival Mr. Plotsky's, I'm afraid my savings wouldn't begin to cover them."

Max pulled a folded document from his case. "This is a list of the claims."

He watched her face lose its color as she silently scrutinized the tally, her gasp loud when she read the final total. Her eyes were enormous as she raised a shocked face to his. "But, but," she stuttered, "this can't be right. I'll never be able to pay this off."

Hiram's *hrump* in the corner went unnoticed as Max felt his reluctant sympathy increase for the struggling young businesswoman. He raised his shoulders almost apologetically. "That's why Mr. Plotsky's offer is so generous, Chrystal. Primarily, he's buying the location. Your entire inventory isn't worth what you owe."

She'd obviously had no idea the amount was so large. With a stunned expression on her face, Chrystal sat silently, the list trembling in her white-knuckled hands.

As if her earlier words had just now been understood, Hiram suddenly rose. "Look, Max, I don't have to take this kinda crap offa nobody. The broad don't wanna sell, she don't wanna sell. Let's just file on her and forget about it."

Max's anger flared. "You agreed that you'd give her a chance. Let her think about the offer, for God's sake."

Hiram's piggy eyes rounded and blinked, then he crammed his cigar back in his mouth. "All right," he conceded then spoke as if Chrystal were not in the room with them, "give her two days, and that's all. I'm waiting downstairs. There ain't enough room in here to far—, uh, breathe." He squeezed around the desk and chair and lumbered into the hallway. A moment later, Max watched his bulky form appear in the showroom downstairs, a trail of hazy smoke following behind him. Max turned back to Chrystal.

Like the curved stem of a wilted flower, her back had slumped against the chair, and she wore a dazed expression. Even though he was just doing what he'd been paid to do, Max suddenly felt like a man with no friends. "Look, Chrystal, we can work this out, I know we can. I've seen cases more hopeless than this one resolved."

"But you don't understand," she said dully. "You just don't understand. I had such dreams, such plans, and now . . ."

Her voice drifted off into such a whisper of sadness that Max wanted to fold her in his arms and tell her he *did* understand. Like a spirit from the past, the thought popped into his mind of paying off her bills. With his income, he could take care of her debts and never look back, but the minute the idea materialized, he banished it, shocked that the whim even took form.

Chrystal's slim shoulders were hunched into her chair, the picture she presented so pitiful, Max felt his natural cynicism return. How could someone be so naive, so innocent? Didn't she realize owning a business was a big undertaking? With effort, he forced his contempt to rise, coating the growing compassion he felt for her with a protective shell of hardness.

He stood abruptly. "You are right, Ms. Cummins, I'm afraid I don't understand, and neither do my clients. Your brother purchased stock from them which they delivered in good faith. The fact that you bought the business without thoroughly checking the books changes nothing for them. They aren't liable for your irresponsibility."

Her head jerked up, and Max instantly wished he could recapture the hateful statement. The words had already left, though, a direct hit. With military precision, her back straightened, and she blinked, her eyes as cold as the Atlantic on a January day.

"You are right about one thing, Mr. Morris. No one takes care of my responsibilities but me."

He nodded once then turned and left. There was nothing else to say.

Chrystal warmed her hands on her third cup of coffee and tried to focus her bleary eyes. The sunlight, streaming in the window at the back of the office, seemed to mock her black mood even as the bright rays promised another perfect California day. With a groan of despair, she leaned back in the battered chair.

For days, she'd searched Neal's records, praying for the impossible, but the receipt for Hiram's stone was not there. Max had to be telling the truth, no matter how much she wanted to deny it, and now her disappointment in Neal welled up inside of her like the late night tide.

Her fingers were sore from punching the buttons on the adding machine, and she winced as she rubbed them over her pounding forehead. After five hours of shuffling her papers, totaling her assets, and cussing her bills, Chrystal was close to admitting the inevitable. She had more debt than she had capital.

Like an unwelcome ghost, her father's presence drifted into the small office, and she involuntarily looked at his tattered recliner, half-way expecting to see him there, shaking his head and mumbling about women who thought they could run a business. She'd tried to ignore the small echo that had been plaguing her since the beginning of this nightmare, but it was difficult to disregard a lifetime of predictions, especially when they appeared to be coming true. Her lips tightened, her anger at her father eclipsed only by her anger at herself and Neal.

Dropping her head into her hands, Chrystal felt a wave of despair wash over her, and for the hundredth time since he'd left her office, she thought about those "courses of action" Max had presented.

None was any more appealing now than it had been earlier, but then earlier, she'd had a glimmer of hope left, false as that faith might have been. Now after more study, the truth of the matter was irrefutable, and she had to make a decision before a choice was made for her.

She could sell out to Hiram Plotsky. The idea made her gag, but so did going to jail. If she let him have the store, she could go somewhere else, start over, but leaving Cummins would validate what her father had always said, and something inside Chrystal simply refused to let her accept what he had always considered to be the truth.

Besides, giving up was not her way of doing things. When she'd told Max she'd never taken the easy road, she'd failed to mention that it'd never been offered. For as long as she could remember, Chrystal had been forced to struggle for what she had, and the idea of turning that over to "Big H" went against all she was.

Fighting back was more her style, but something told her that wouldn't be wise this time. Maxwell Morris looked too proficient. He'd annihilate any attorney she could afford, and in the end, she'd lose more than she stood to pay out. She had to admit he'd probably given her pretty good advice; a battle would cost everyone.

The only option left was paying everyone off, and Chrystal knew she couldn't do that. Abruptly she stood, needing the movement, the action, as if the energy would recirculate her thinking as well as her blood. She went downstairs to the not yet open store.

Chrystal tried to attribute the moisture in her eyes to the brilliance of the sunlight pouring into the showroom, but she couldn't lie to herself. Blind with tears, she stumbled around the empty cases, remembering how she'd felt when the sale had been completed, and the store was finally her own. Proud, happy, ready to prove to herself and the world that she *could* run a business.

Now the dream was crumbling to dust, and no matter how hard she held on, she couldn't seem to contain all the particles as they slipped through her fingers, out of control. Mr. Meyer's melee, Mrs. Meriweather's emeralds, Hiram Plotsky's diamond, Maxwell Morris's options—they all blended together and then shifted, spiraling downwards. Her aspirations joined her problems in a sad little pile of ashes.

The day passed like any other with one major difference: Nothing seemed to matter. Chrystal sold a nice one carat solitaire to a giggling young couple, an older man bought a lovely diamond pin for a fiftieth wedding anniversary, and a stern young woman dressed in a severe navy business suit came in and left with a heavy gold chain for herself. "To celebrate my promotion," she'd said gruffly.

Chrystal knew their sales, while all good, wouldn't help, and in a further fit of despair, all she could do was compare her failures to their successes. She'd devoted her whole life to buying the store so she had no one special; there was no hope of an engagement ring for her, much less an anniversary pin. And the businesswoman, she really rubbed salt into Chrystal's wounded ego.

With weary disappointment, she locked up, grateful the horrible day had finally ended. She wanted to go home and crawl into bed, pull the covers over her head, and pretend that nothing had happened. Chrystal knew she was wallowing in her pity, but she couldn't seem to help herself. There was no way she could pay off everyone, and selling out to Hiram was beginning to look like the only real option.

By the time she reached her condo, her shoulders were tight with tension, and she groaned aloud when she remembered her haughty words: *I take care of all my responsibilities. Hah! I can't take care of any of them!*

Her shoes came off first, and then the austere black dress she'd worn to match her mood. Reaching into her closet, Chrystal pulled out the rattiest robe she could find and thrust her arms into its reassuring warmth. Her hair slid down her back as she pulled out the pins, then she shook her head, trying to loosen her neck and the gloomy thoughts that seemed lodged in her brain. The movement only aggravated her headache.

Shuffling into the kitchen, she opened the refrigerator and leaned her elbow on the door, staring dismally into its empty depths.

Just as she reached into the coldness for the last carton of cherry yogurt, the doorbell rang. *Oh great,* she moaned, *just what I need, someone trying to sell me something*. She slammed the door shut and walked through the den to the small, marble-tiled entry. Stretching upward, she pressed her eye against the peephole then gasped and fell back down, clutching the collar of her robe as if it could offer her some protection from the man on the other side of the door.

Maxwell Morris! What in the world did he want? Her panic-stricken eyes automatically darted to the mirror nearby. Her hair hung in wild tendrils around eyes ringed in fatigue, and the housecoat she wore should have gone to Goodwill five years ago. Why hadn't he come to the shop? Why here? Why now?

She thought about ignoring the demand produced by his finger on the bell, but she couldn't; that went against her nature. She couldn't ignore the noise any more than she could her responsibilities for Neal.

With a moan, she ran her fingers through her hair then tightened the belt on her dressing gown. Taking a deep breath, she cracked the door, leaving the chain on.

"Chrystal?" Max asked, "I know you probably don't want to see me, but we need to talk. I thought, well, I . . ."

She slammed the door, then instantly reopened it, the chain banging against the side. Silently, she stood in the portal, knowing the look that creased her forehead was as belligerent as her voice but not caring. "What do you want now?"

"I brought a peace offering," he said, holding out a white plastic bag and ignoring her question. "May I come in?"

Casual slacks and a black cotton sweater made him appear younger and less intimidating than the thousand dollar suits he usually wore. The ponytail was gone. Long, dark hair framed his face, somehow softening the severe angles and planes, emphasizing instead his full lips and dark eyes.

Stunned by his unexpected appearance, Chrystal tried to analyze her immediate, overwhelming response but failed. Maxwell Morris was simply the most seductive man she'd ever met.

She told herself she shouldn't, but tantalizing odors were drifting to her from the sack he held, and when he held out his other hand, full of the most beautiful tulips she'd ever laid eyes on, she opened the door wider and stepped aside. Max walked inside and quickly closed the door, as if he was afraid she might change her mind at the last minute.

He handed her the flowers, accepted her thanks, and followed her into a small dining room, placing the sack on the table. She stood, clutching the long, green stems in her hands as he removed the still steaming cartons. "Vegetable dumplings, General Tso's chicken, moo shi pork—with pancakes—pork fried rice, Phoenix shrimp—"

"My God, Max, you brought enough food to feed the entire Chinese army. I do live alone, you know."

His boyish smile suddenly transformed his face, and the stern, forbidding attorney metamorphosed into an ordinary man, eager to please, anxious to impress. Chrystal's stomach took a funny tumble that had nothing to do with the feast on her table.

"Yes," he said slowly, "I do know that, and I'm glad, too."

Part of her urged caution while the other side was thrilled. There could only be one reason he was happy she lived alone, and it wasn't because he didn't want to share the meal he'd just brought. She looked down at the pale, peach flowers in her hands then lifted her eyes to his. "They're beautiful."

"I'm glad you like them." His black eyes pierced her.

Even as he answered, she felt her guard go up. They were adversaries, and mutual admiration wouldn't change that, would it? No, she cautioned herself, Max wanted something, she just didn't yet know what.

She swallowed hard and broke his stare then went to the cabinet and removed a vase, quickly placing the flowers and water in it, as though the stems were beginning to burn her fingers. She reached into the cabinet once more and took down two delicate china plates.

"Tea?"

"That would be nice."

The kettle banged against the side of the sink, then the water gushed. A few seconds later, she strode back to the table. "It's almost boiling," she said.

"Fine."

He sat down and crossed his legs, looking casually around the kitchen. Her feelings of defensiveness grew. Under his curious scrutiny, the room seemed to shrink, and beneath her façade of politeness, barely concealed irritation began to simmer like the water on the stove. Was his appearance now some kind of ruse? He'd looked innocent at first in her store, too.

At his studied nonchalance, her anxiety ballooned until she could no longer contain herself. "Why did you really come here? Did somebody else decide they want a piece of me?"

He looked genuinely startled. "No, nothing like that. I just felt like we'd gotten off on a bad beginning, and I wanted to start over. Hiram didn't help matters, either. Sometimes he can be overwhelming—"

"Overwhelming?" she interrupted. "How about obnoxious?"

"That, too, but he is my client and frankly I shouldn't even be here."

"What do you mean?"

"My first responsibility is to Hiram, not to you, Chrystal. I should be letting you worry about what's going to happen next, not sharing a cozy dinner—"

"This is not—"

He held up his hand, and she snapped her mouth shut as he continued. "To be honest, however, we thought it best to move forward with all possible speed and ignore the usual client/attorney aspect of this problem. Actually, I'm helping Hiram out as a friend more than as his attorney anyway, and I'd like to do the same for you. These things have a way of snowballing, and if you can handle them quickly they don't seem to gain as much force."

The boyish smile and casual attire faded into the background. Once they'd started talking business, he was the successful attorney again; in fact, Chrystal now wondered if she hadn't imagined the way his dark eyes had warmed her a moment ago. She met his gaze with an antagonistic look. "I wouldn't think you'd be interested in stopping the avalanche. More time, more money, isn't that how your business works?"

His voice turned neutral. "Not all attorneys are blood-suckers, Chrystal. Some of us are actually pretty fair-minded individuals."

She raised her eyebrows then rose as the kettle whistled. A few seconds later, she returned with thin, handle-less cups and a teapot on a small tray. Wordlessly, she poured the steaming Darjeeling as he filled their plates.

He picked up the ebony chopsticks she'd laid earlier beside the plate, hesitated, then abruptly dropped them. "I'm worried about you, Chrystal, and I want to help." He reached across the table for her hand, but she pretended not to notice and grabbed her own chopsticks instead. Apparently undaunted, he turned his hands palm-side up in a gesture of openness. "I'm not out to destroy what you've accomplished, believe me. I understand what your business means to you."

The dumpling she had halfway to her mouth stopped. "You don't understand anything about this, Max."

"You feel that way right now, but I *do* want to help you. If we work together, I honestly think we can solve the problem, but if you go out and hire an attorney of your own, only he and I will end up with the money."

She dropped her own chopsticks, the dumpling sliding across her plate. "Money! That's definitely what all this is about, isn't it? Money, money, money. That's all you and Mr. Plotsky see. Who gets paid, who doesn't. What's the bottom line? The final figure, that's the only thing that counts, right?"

She stood up, throwing her napkin to the table top. "What about my dreams? What about my hopes? I've wanted to own that store since I was eight years old. I planned, I worked, I saved, and finally, despite my father's predictions and my brother's inheritance, I managed to buy it."

She took a deep breath and felt her legs quiver. "Now, you march in here and tell me if I don't cooperate, you're going to take it over. Why should I be thrilled with that?''

"I'm not saying you should be thril—"

"Frankly, I think I'm entitled to a little anger."

"Of course," he instantly agreed. "Why, I'd be outraged if I were you." He blinked, his bewilderment obvious. "In fact, if I were you, I'd be out of here, and on the first plane to wherever in the hell it is your brother ran off to, looking for a piece of his skin."

Her knuckles turned white as she gripped the back of her chair. His agreement was expected, but his understanding touched her in a way she wasn't expecting, triggering her to share more revelations than she'd planned. "That's exactly what I want to do, but I can't." Her voice suddenly cracked. "I can't because this is all my fault." She dropped her head and whispered again. "It's all my fault."

For two seconds, he studied her face then rose and started toward her. She held a hand out in front of her as if to stop him, but he wouldn't stop, he kept coming, and Chrystal recognized the intent in his eyes. She knew if he touched her, she'd break down. She fled into the den.

She blindly stumbled to the window in the dimly lit room, wishing she'd kept her mouth shut. *Why had she told him that?* Mortified and embarrassed, she prayed Max would have the grace to leave her alone, to let her suffer in silence.

But he didn't.

When he spoke, his voice was a whisper by her ear. "You're making a mistake," he said softly. "I don't know why, but you're making a mistake."

His closeness disturbed her almost as much as his words. She swirled, her face a mask of resentment.

"No, you're the one making a mistake. You can't help me, no one can because this is my responsibility, my moral obligation."

"Chrystal, I don't understand why you are taking this so personally. Business is business, you know that. Yes, technically, you are responsible, but morally? Why do you say that?"

Their faces were inches apart. The harsh light from the street lamp outside added to the single lamp's glow, revealing the genuine concern in Max's eyes. She hesitated. Talking about her past was painful, and she didn't really want to expose her more vulnerable side, but she'd gone this far, she might as well finish.

"I raised Neal. Our mother died shortly after he was born, and my father turned him over to me."

"But you were only a kid yourself."

She shrugged. "Yes, but what was I supposed to do? Argue? Dad was so wrapped up in the shop that he couldn't see what was happening. Looking back now, I realize he worked to forget—to forget Mother, us, reality." Chrystal smiled sadly. "All those things that make up life, I guess."

"Pretty unfair, if you ask me."

"I didn't mind that much. Until I reached high school, I thought my life was like everyone else's." She dropped her eyes, her voice barely concealing her regrets. "Unfortunately, there I learned otherwise. I found out that the other girls didn't have to miss their proms to take care of little brothers with the measles. Instead of running home after school and starting dinner, they went to the local drive-in and had Cokes with their boyfriends or went to cheerleading practice or just goofed off, little things I never had time for."

Max lifted his hand to her face and smoothed a strand of hair away from her eyes. The comforting touch was more than she could handle, and she tried to hide her face, but he put his hands on her shoulders and stopped her.

"Those aren't what I'd call 'little things,' Chrystal. You sacrificed your childhood for Neal's."

The tears in her eyes stung as much as his words, but she had to face them both. Once acknowledged, her revelation seemed to have a life of its own, and the feelings of resentment she'd thought were long buried rose to the surface like irrepressible bubbles.

"Yes, I did," she cried, "but I had no other choice. I was the older, everyone depended on me. If I didn't cook, we didn't eat. If I didn't wash the clothes, there were none to wear." Her voice rose. "I didn't have a choice, Max. If I didn't do those things, they didn't get done. Don't you understand that?"

Before she could protest, Max wrapped his arms around her and pulled her into his chest. With one hand, he stroked her back, and with his other, he smoothed her hair, murmuring softly all the while. "Shh, shh."

His comforting arms were a shock. For one strange moment, Chrystal felt as if she'd found something she hadn't known she'd lost, and the feeling left her so surprised she didn't know what to do. Instantly, the tensions of the past and the uncertainty of the future seemed overwhelming. She found herself sobbing against Max's sweater. The tears flowed copiously, and the release they brought was something she'd never felt before. She hurt so much though, she couldn't stop.

With his arms still around her, he led her to the

nearby sofa and sat, pulling her down beside him. Chrystal was so upset, the only protest she could manage was a hiccup which he ignored as he pressed her head against him, his arms tight around her shoulders. "It's okay," he whispered.

Mindlessly she continued. "I, I tried to do the best that I could, but I *was* only a kid. Neal was so stubborn, too. He wouldn't listen. He insisted on having things his way all the time, and besides that, even when he was a baby, he was so cute, so charming, that I gave him whatever he wanted. I didn't know what else to do."

"Good grief, Chrystal, how could you do differently? Hell, if you ask me, most parents don't do such a hot job raising their kids. How were you supposed to do better?"

His words made sense, but for too many years Chrystal had blamed herself for every wrong Neal did. The arguments were part of her, so she ignored Max's logic. "I was old enough, I just didn't do a good job."

He shook his head but said nothing and cradled her once more, rocking back and forth as she continued to cry softly. Beneath her wet cheek, the soft cotton sweater he wore absorbed her tears as easily as his comforting warmth soaked up her pain. The steel like arms around her heaving shoulders were a safe harbor against the storm of her emotions, but even as she reveled in their protection, she found the feeling evolving into something else, something even more powerful. She tried to pull away from their refuge, delayed chagrin flaming her face, but his gentle hold tightened imperceptibly.

"I, I don't make it a habit of crying in front of

strangers," she said, dabbing her face with the spotless handkerchief he magically produced.

"I'm not a stranger," he said softly. "If you'd let me, I'd like to be your friend."

She raised her eyes from behind the square of soft linen. "Why?" she asked hoarsely. "Two weeks ago, you didn't even know me, then after we met, you thought I was a thief. Now you want to help me. Why?"

The finger he raised to trace the line of her jaw trembled. "Let's just say something about you brings out my better side."

"That's not good enough, Max. Why? Why do you want to help?"

"Do you have to have the answer to everything? Just accept it and the fact that I think you're a beautiful woman who's intelligent and bright but has a blind spot where her brother's concerned and needs some help."

Her protest was silenced as he put a finger to her lips. His touch stopped her breath. Suddenly, she felt as though a switch had been thrown on for her senses, and an overwhelming awareness of their closeness electrified her. The hard muscles beneath his soft sweater, the expensive smell of French-milled soap, the hot dark eyes on her face all came together. Her breasts, rising and falling with her quickened breath, seemed to grow suddenly warm, and she became aware that she wore nothing under her robe but a skimpy black teddy.

His eyes changed as they stared into hers, then his hands left her face to rest on either side of her neck. Inevitably, inescapably, he drew her deeper into his embrace, and she felt helpless to resist. When his lips claimed hers, she was willing but not ready.

His kiss was like flying without a plane. She felt her senses soar and leave her mundane concerns behind as his mouth possessed hers, his fingers gently massaging her neck. Her pulse was all that seemed to remain, pounding in her ears like a roaring wind.

The touch of his lips destroyed any myths she'd ever harbored about kissing. This wasn't a loving, gentle caress; it was a revolution, an insurrection, anarchy of the senses, and it liberated all of Chrystal's feelings.

He continued his arousing torture, and just as she thought she'd die if he stopped and die if he didn't, his onslaught diminished into a teasing, lighter trace, his tongue feathering across her lips, leaving a trail of fiery sensation.

A searing heat built in her chest and radiated outward, smothering her with desire and confusion. What was wrong with her? How could she respond like this to a man determined to destroy her?

Flustered and floundering, Chrystal pushed Max away and jumped up, before she could change her mind. Clutching her collar about her neck, Chrystal didn't need a mirror to know her face was bright red.

"I, I—"

He stood up slowly but did not move any closer. "What's wrong? Don't tell me you haven't been kissed before."

"Well, of course not," she said stiffly. "But I don't want you to think I do this all the time. I mean, today was a really horrible day, and I, I, I'm sorry," she finished lamely.

"Sorry for what?" he said. "Because you let your hair down and cried a little? Because you told me about your past? Because you let me comfort you?"

He grinned that devastating grin again, and this time Chrystal was expecting the flutter she felt in her lower body. "You don't need to apologize for anything," his liquid voice dropped again, "especially for the latter."

She ignored his implication; it was the only way she could handle him. Her back straightened. "I was simply indicating my regret for, for acting so unprofessional. You were kind in coming here, bringing me food, listening to me complain."

"I'd like to be more than just 'kind' to you, Chrystal. I want more than that."

His kiss had told her that already, but, perversely, knowing she'd never give in, she wanted to hear the words of persuasion anyway. "Like what?"

"What do you think?" His voice was brandy-warm, a deep rumble that flowed across the room and enveloped her.

"I'm not sure," she lied, trying to resist the magnetic pull of his tones.

"Not sure about us or not sure about what I want?"

She realized Max wouldn't settle for less than the truth. "Both," she whispered.

"All right," he growled, "how about this? I want to make love to you—all night long—till we're both exhausted, then I want to wake up beside you and see the morning sun in your hair. I want to taste your eyelids, and kiss your—"

"Max," she stopped him, her heart pounding so loud she was afraid it would jump out of her chest. "I can't give you any more than kindness, not right now."

"Why?"

"You know why."

He took two steps closer to her, and she automatically pulled her robe closer, her hands forming a barrier of protection between them.

"If you're talking about business, I don't give a damn what Hiram, or anyone else thinks, and as long as he gets his pound of flesh, he's happy."

"Yes," she cried suddenly, seizing the excuse. "That's exactly what I mean. His pound of flesh is coming off me, don't you see?"

"That's crazy, Chrystal. This is your brother's problem, not yours. Let me find him, and make him face the music this time."

"No, I already said I was responsible, not Neal." She ran a hand through her hair distractedly. "This is what I mean, Max. Right here. We can't possibly build a relationship out of such discord."

Max stilled her agitation by gripping her shoulders in both of his hands. Like two hot coals, his black eyes burned his expression into her memory, and Chrystal knew she'd never be able to forget his look. "Maybe, but don't you ever gamble? Take a chance that something wonderful might happen?"

"No," she said instantly. "Not this time, Max. I can't."

His intensity seared her into silence. For two short heartbeats, she was sure he was going to kiss her again, but he abruptly dropped his hands, spun around, and strode to the door. Gripping the knob, he stopped and turned once more, his look trapping her in a web of promised passion. "All right, then, I'll leave you alone—for now."

The door closed softly behind him, leaving her breathless, confused, and very disappointed.

FOUR

The following day, Max's mind refused to focus on the confusion of legal briefs strewn over his desk or the appointments he'd already scheduled. Even the blond divorcée he'd arranged to see over lunch couldn't hold his attention. All he could think of was Chrystal.

The soft lips he'd kissed the night before, the eyes swimming in tears, the rigid straightness in her back—she was so full of contradictions that the more he thought of her, the more intrigued he became.

By the time he got home, the California afternoon had turned cold, and as he tossed the match toward the kindling in the fireplace, his thoughts returned once more to Chrystal Cummins. She reminded him of a rare orchid—a fragile bloom that might bend in the face of adversity, but would never break.

His mother had possessed that kind of strength. She'd lost two other children after she'd had Max, yet he'd never seen her cry. Even as a child, he'd wondered about that fortitude—that ability to face what must have been the tragedy of her heart and still do what had to be done. When he'd left home and gone to college, his father's eyes had glistened, but his mother had simply smiled and kissed him goodbye. He'd always known she loved him, though, and the silence of her approval had almost made that love even more special.

She allowed herself to show more emotion, but in her own way, Chrystal was just as strong as his mother—and twice as protective. He'd never seen anyone react like she had when he'd questioned her about Neal. Max stared pensively into the developing fire, the flames glowing blue and red against the blackened brick. Why? Why shed tears for a brother who obviously didn't care?

Neal Cummins sounded like the biggest jerk in the world, and just thinking about him made Max's confusion flash into anger. Chrystal had absolutely no reason in the world to take on her brother's responsibilities, so why did she insist on claiming them for herself?

With a snort of disgust, Max turned and strode to the wet bar at one end of the living room. Reaching into the upper cabinet, he grabbed a tumbler then filled it with ice, the cubes clinking hollowly against the crystal. The amber whiskey splashed over the edge as he added water from the tap.

As he tilted his head and swallowed half the contents of the drink, his eyes passed over a photograph of his parents sitting on the marble counter top. He picked up the silver frame and walked to the wall of windows that made up one side of the room, cradling his glass in his other hand. The soft California sunset gave him just enough light to see the faces of the only two people he'd ever really loved.

In the picture, they stood close together in a small garden behind the house of Max's childhood. They'd run a small florist shop, and growing plants was the passion of their lives; the garden attested to it. In front of a backdrop of flowers, with their arms wrapped around each other, they smiled into the camera, his mother's face shaded by a large straw hat, his father's cap pulled down over his forehead. Max had taken the photograph more than ten years ago, but when he closed his eyes briefly the scent of a thousand roses filled his mind. Two years later, his mother had suffered a fatal heart attack and one year after that, his father had simply given up and joined her.

Slowly, Max opened his eyes and sighed. The day his father had died, Max had felt so abandoned that he had found himself wishing once more for the sisters and brothers his mother had carried but lost—something he hadn't done in many, many years. If they'd been alive, he'd thought then, they could have shared his grief—maybe divided it into manageable pieces. As it was, Max had carried the heavy burden entirely on his own.

In the empty room behind him, the fire popped suddenly, dragging Max back to the present. Sipping again from the now watery drink, he turned his back to the windows and moved once more toward the fire. Placing the photo on the glass-topped coffee table in front of the sofa, Max paused.

If Neal was my brother, how would I feel now?

Max's glass stopped halfway to his open mouth. Without taking a drink, he lowered the glass and looked once more into the fire as though the flames would tell him a truth different from the one now filling his mind.

Of course, he'd help his own brother. That was a tie too strong for anything to break. Max's lips tightened. He might help but he wouldn't take responsibility, he answered himself grimly.

Yes, but what if he'd raised that brother? What if that brother was more like his child than his sibling?

Max sat down heavily on the couch and cradled the crystal glass between his hands. In his heart, he knew the answer. He might not take Chrystal's unwavering stance, but he *would* feel some kind of loyalty—some thread of connection—it'd be impossible not to.

The fire had finally begun to warm the big den. Max lifted his face to the glowing warmth, and his eyes were instantly drawn to the picture of his parents. The reflection of the fire's flames danced across their faces, granting the motionless couple the appearance of life once more. His mother seemed to smile, his father to nod his head.

Max squeezed his eyes closed. Whether Chrystal liked it or not, he was going to try to find Neal Cummins. It was the right thing to do.

Chrystal stared at the piles of diamonds in front of her, her tweezers poised in one hand and her loupe idle in the other. She'd sorted the same packet of melee twice now, and each time she couldn't even tell when she'd finished. The diamonds should have been graded by color and clarity, but her mind simply wasn't on the task that usually soothed her, and the results were apparent.

She wished the other decisions facing her were just as self-evident, but they weren't. They were questions with no answers, choices with no solutions, decisions with no relief, and Maxwell Morris seemed determined to make the difficult, impossible.

Rising from the sorting table, Chrystal rolled her tense neck and stared at the vase of tulips he'd given her. Bringing the pale peach blooms to the office had been a mistake—Max's kiss was already haunting her like an ill-mannered demon, and she didn't need a more visible reminder. If she couldn't exorcise its memory, the sleepless night she'd spent last night would be the first of many. She pulled in her bottom lip and stared out the window beside her, but she didn't see the bright afternoon scene. Instead, she saw a pair of dark, understanding eyes looking down at her with sympathy and something else—something she wasn't ready to acknowledge, even if he was.

They disagreed on more than one thing, too. He obviously didn't understand the obligations Chrystal still felt towards Neal. In fact, she wasn't sure *she* understood the complicated sense of loyalty and disillusionment thoughts of Neal always produced, but he was her brother, and she didn't want anyone criticizing him.

For the moment, however, what she needed to manage was paying the bills. She pulled her hand through her hair and felt the frustrations well to an almost unmanageable level. Max would be returning soon, and if she didn't have some plan of her own, she'd be forced to accept Hiram's offer.

Maybe she *should* go to the legal clinic. A second opinion never hurt, but she hated the thought of going there. Somehow, that action seemed to validate her dilemma, make the reality more critical, even confirm Neal's deceit and her failure.

The door to the office opened, and Marion slipped

inside. "Here's the mail," she said tossing the pile of catalogs and letters on Chrystal's desk.

Chrystal's eyes went warily to the envelope Marion still held in her hand. "Not another bill, I hope?"

Marion smiled. "No, an invitation." She handed the heavy creme envelope to Chrystal, her long, red-tipped nails gleaming. "From that retailer you met at the last jewelry show, you know, Johnson's over in Carmel?"

Chrystal nodded and removed the card from the gold-lined envelope. "Classy stationary," she said and looked up at Marion, an envious gleam in her eye. "Business must be good in Carmel."

"Wait till you read the invite."

Chrystal quickly scanned the heavy black script, her eyebrows raising while she read aloud the short note Warden Johnson had written at the bottom of the invitation. "Wish you could come. Have all the big suppliers from New York arriving to show their wares. Have ordered extra receipts printed."

Grudging admiration slipped into her voice. "Warden's having a 'sales' party. I read about a store in New York that did this once on Valentine's Day. The owner invited special suppliers with exotic inventory, then invited everyone in town who had any money, and plied them with drinks and food until they parted with the contents of their wallets. Sounds like Warden's trying the same thing." She raised her face to Marion's. "God, I'd love to do something like that!"

Marion looked at her sharply. "Dream on. You've got some other things to think about right now."

"Yes, but, Marion, do you know how much we could make? Have champagne and caviar, invite all the local big spenders? You know the rich, they'll come to anything with free booze and food.''

"But somebody's got to pay for all that and—''

"Don't be so cynical, Marion,'' Chrystal chided. "You have to spend a little to make a lot. I think it's a marvelous idea, and I bet Warden's going to make tons of money. I wonder . . .''

"Oh no, you don't. You don't wonder anything. You know you can't spend money on something like that right now. Maxwell Morris would have a heart attack. You owe everyone in town, what would that look like, throwing a big party?''

Chrystal's exasperation lifted her voice. "Marion, who cares? I'm so far gone, it doesn't even matter. In fact, this might be the solution to our problems.'' Her cheeks flushed with sudden excitement. "If we had a major event here, here in the store, and invited everyone who's anyone, we could really clean up, especially if I could get a special supplier, like CeCe, to bring extra inventory, pieces no one around here has seen before, really different things. Don't you think it'd work?''

"Are you crazy, Chrystal? Even if you could get that nutty woman out here, things like this cost scads of money, which you don't have.'' She looked at Chrystal, her concern obviously growing. "Besides, who would you invite? We have pretty good traffic here, but let's face it, Harry Winston, we're not. The really big spenders have never come to Cummins.''

"Well, I'm going to change that.'' Her pale eyes narrowed, and Chrystal raised a single finger. "What about Mrs. Meriweather? She shops here, and you can't say she isn't high society.''

Marion held up her hands in mock disgust. "One client, Chrystal, she's one client. I admit, she's a good one, even buying jewelry for that piddling, damned dog of hers, but she couldn't carry the whole party.''

"No, but she'd help. If I got her support, she'd tell all her friends, and those people have money coming out their—"

The phone jangled, interrupting Chrystal's growing eagerness. Marion shook her head, her long braids swaying as if they agreed with her pessimism. Chrystal reached for the phone as Marion continued to grouse.

"No way," Marion muttered, "no way. If he were still alive, your father would have a stroke. . . .''

Chrystal's fingers tightened on the receiver as Marion's words drifted back to her. If her father were still alive, they wouldn't be in the fix they were in, she thought guiltily. Now she had to get them out of it.

"Cummins," she barked into the phone.

"Chrystal Cummins, please.''

Something about the way the man said her name made her think he'd rather be talking to someone else, and a sudden shiver of foreboding ran down her spine.

"Speaking."

"Ms. Cummins, my name is Bob Grene, I'm with the Jewelers Commerce Association.''

Chrystal clutched the phone with instantly sweaty hands. The association was the watchdog of the industry; their word provided credit, name recognition, everything essential in a business based on trust. She had a bad feeling.

"What can I do for you, Mr. Grene?"

"We've had an inquiry about your store, and I

wanted to inform you before I released the information. Do you know a Mr. Maxwell Morris?''

Her stomach tightened, and an angry flush darkened her face. "Yes, I know him," she answered tautly. "What exactly does Mr. Morris want to know?''

"Well, the usual, your payment history, your rating by the association, that sort of thing, but he also had some more unusual questions, and we generally don't release that kind of report until the jeweler knows.''

"More unusual?''

"Yes, Mr. Morris also asked us if we knew where Neal Cummins was. He wanted some information on your brother and the status of the business when he purchased it. Actually, we had tried to call Mr. Cummins at the last number he gave us, but it had been disconnected. We wanted to update our records anyway, so I thought I'd call you and find out. I hope you don't mind.''

"No," she answered, her blood beginning to boil. "I don't mind, as a matter of fact, I'm delighted that you called. My brother is out of the country at the moment, but I'll see that Mr. Morris gets his answers.''

"Then shall we release the report?''

"Do I have a choice?''

"As a matter of fact, I'm afraid not, Ms. Cummins. We're simply informing you as a courtesy. Since Mr. Morris is a well-known attorney, it behooves us to be agreeable." A short pause crackled down the line. "I'm sure you can appreciate that fact," he said contritely.

Her voice was ironic. "Oh yes," she said, "I do understand your position.''

He rang off, and Chrystal banged the receiver into the cradle. *What in the hell did Maxwell Morris think he was doing now?* She'd told him she would take care of the situation. It was her responsibility. Why was he trying to hunt down Neal?

All her maternal instincts rose to the surface, and along with them Chrystal felt her animosity rise. Neal had made a big mistake, yes, but if Maxwell Morris thought he'd track her brother down and make him suffer for that misjudgment, then he'd made a bigger one.

"You're making a big mistake, buddy-boy." Hiram looked at Max through a fog of cigar smoke. "You gotta think with your brain, not with your—"

Max held up his hands to stop the flow of words. "I *am* thinking, Hiram, and with nothing *but* my head. Chrystal Cummins has run that store successfully for months. I believe she will continue to do so and will eventually pay you back—if we let her stay in business."

With a stubborn snap, Hiram's teeth clamped down on the soggy end of his cigar. "She's got a smart mouth on her."

Max felt his eyes go wide in amazement. "And that bothers you? My God, Hiram, have you listened to yourself lately?"

He yanked the cigar from his mouth and pointed it at Max. "How I talk is none of your concern. You better be watching your own business, if you know what I mean."

Max knew most of Hiram's threats were pointless—more bluff than anything else—but something about his tone of voice stopped the protest forming in the back of Max's mind. "What are you saying, Hiram?"

From behind his desk, Hiram raised the first of his two chins and looked down his nose at Max. His small, black eyes glittered with maliciousness. "How do I know you're working in my best interests?"

Confusion pulled Max's eyebrows together. "What in the hell does that mean? I'm your attorney, aren't I?"

"Yeah, but it looks to me like your interest in the delightful Ms. Cummins is more than business."

Max stared at the corpulent man behind the desk in surprise. "Who told you that?"

Hiram pulled his full, wet lips back in what passed for a smile. "I got my eyes, don't I? I saw the way you were looking her over at the store the other day." He waved the cigar in a circle like a child would a sparkler on the Fourth of July. "Seems like there's a potential for conflict of interest, if you ask me. I'm paying you for this. I want my money's worth."

Max stared at him, briefly lost in thought. Actually, he'd considered this very fact after leaving Chrystal's house the other night, but he'd dismissed the idea as inconsequential. He'd always do the best job he could for everyone involved, and if the situation changed and that became impossible, he'd make sure Chrystal and Hiram both knew. In this case, however, it didn't matter because all the parties had consented to the unusual situation. He wasn't even representing either one of them, for that matter. The payment schedule he was going to draw up was something any accountant could have done in ten minutes. Hiram, however, didn't know that.

Max rubbed his chin as if in deep thought. "You

know, Hiram, you might have a good point there. I hadn't really thought about it in those terms.''

Hiram sucked on his cigar and nodded his head, obviously pleased. He smoked in silence for a few moments, then Max watched as Hiram's eyes grew smaller and his mouth tighter.

''If I don't pay you, are you still representing me?''

Max faked a frown of concern then nimbly sidestepped the issue. ''I can't do this work for free, Hiram. I've got bills, pro bono cases, my office, not to mention the clinic—''

Hiram rolled the cigar to one side of his mouth and held up his hand. The heavy, gold rings he wore flashed under the bright office lights. ''All right, all right—''

''You might have an idea there, though, Hiram.'' Max chewed his bottom lip as though his thought had been triggered by Hiram's proposal. ''How about a trade instead?''

Like a giant bullfrog, Hiram blinked twice before answering. Max knew he had him hooked, but the wily jeweler was too savvy a trader to immediately say yes.

''Like what?'' he finally asked.

''Do you need a tax break?''

''Does a bear live in the woods? Hell, yes. You ought to know that.''

Max nodded. He always accompanied Hiram on his perennial trip to the Internal Revenue Service. Max leaned closer to the desk as if he were about to impart a secret. ''Why don't you donate my fee to my newest project down by the clinic? You'll get the write-off, the center will get the money, and I won't have to worry about any conflict between representing you and Chrystal. How does that sound?"

Max watched as Hiram fought back a grin. He obviously loved the idea, but Max would never hear him say so. The jeweler leaned back in his chair and nonchalantly studied the ash growing on his cigar. "Well, about that fee—let's talk dollars, here, Morris. . . ."

"But it's not even a diamond. Why should a ruby cost so much?"

"Burmese stones of this quality are extremely rare, Mrs. Smythe," Chrystal explained patiently. "This is as close to 'pigeon's blood' as I've seen in a long time."

" 'Pigeon's blood' Yuck! What does that mean?"

Chrystal grinned. "It's a jeweler's term that refers to the deep red color of some rubies." With the tweezers in her right hand, she picked up the loose stone and placed the ruby gently on top of the fingers of her left hand. The sunlight coming through the window sparkled off the facets as she moved her hand slowly.

"This is really a superb stone," she murmured, almost as if to herself. "The cushion cut always looks so stunning paired with diamond trillions on either side. I'd use eighteen carat gold, of course, and —"

"Trillions? You aren't talking about those triangle-shaped diamonds, are you? They always look so small." Mrs. Smythe's voice died off in a high-pitched whine as she pulled her eyes away from the ruby to stare at Chrystal.

Startled, Chrystal glanced up and remembered who she was talking to. Margaret Smythe had come in twice before and both times she'd bought large, flashy rings.

"You know, you're absolutely correct, Mrs. Smythe. I wasn't really thinking straight." Chrystal smiled brightly. "Perhaps surrounding the ruby with brilliant, uh, round diamonds, would be better. Maybe even pave them in a dome. What do you think?"

The well-known plastic surgeon's wife grinned broadly, her smooth face pulling back. "Now that sounds more like it. Maybe some fancy gold filigree down the side. . . ."

Chrystal swallowed a groan and put the stone on the velvet pad lying on the counter, reaching for the pad and pencil she kept under the counter. Quickly she began sketching with broad sure strokes as the plump woman before her ohhed and ahhed. In twenty minutes, Chrystal had the design down and the sale made.

Mrs. Smythe left the store happily, and Chrystal retreated to the office.

"That sounded interesting," Marion teased.

"Oh yes, Mrs. Smythe has a real eye. She knows exactly what will look the worst but," Chrystal lifted her hands and eyes, "who am I to argue? With a checkbook that big, she can have anything she wants. Dr. Smythe only has to do one more nip and tuck, and she's got a new bauble."

Marion dropped her head and looked at Chrystal over the rim of the half-glasses she wore. "Do I detect a note of envy in that smooth voice of yours?"

Chrystal flopped into her chair with an uncharacteristic lack of finesse and grimaced. "Oh, Marion, is it that obvious?" She let her head fall back and stared at the ceiling. "I'm sorry, but every time I make a sale, I think 'How much can I make from this? Will it help? Who can I pay off?' Isn't that terrible? I never thought about money like that before. Now when I see these rich women come in here, all I can think about is how they could pay off my bills with their monthly clothes budget.'' Her gray eyes clouded with guilt. ''Isn't that awful?''

Marion's sympathy wrinkled her forehead as she pulled off her glasses. ''No, honey, that's not awful at all. What's awful is the way that damned brother of yours left you to deal with all this.''

Chrystal's tightened jaw revealed her displeasure, but Marion continued. ''Don't look at me like that. I don't care what you think, he did you wrong, and I can't believe you're putting up with it.'' She shook her head, the heavy gold loops she wore in her ears swinging with the movement. ''I don't understand you, Chrystal. When you weren't much bigger than him, you'd take the blame when he knocked over the glass of milk. Why, I remember once when he got a 'C' in math, you told your father Neal's teacher just didn't like him, and that's why he hadn't gotten an 'A.' '' She pursed her lips, disgust drawing lines from her nose to her mouth. ''The truth is Neal never gave a damn then, and he doesn't now, and you're still standing up for him.''

''That's enough, Marion,'' Chrystal said sharply. Neal wasn't perfect by any stretch of the imagination, but Marion's criticism really rankled. ''You don't understand—''

''Oh, I understand plenty, girl. You're the one that's confused on this one.''

''Marion . . .''

Chrystal's warning disappeared into the air as Marion waved her scarlet-tipped nails in the air. ''Just like you're confused on that damn party idea. Oh, yeah, I saw those brochures on your desk from Luther's. He's the caterer you used at Christmas, isn't he? You're thinking about having a party, aren't you? Don't lie to me."

"All I did was call the man, Marion, for goodness sakes. I haven't made up my mind yet. Don't be so close-minded."

"Right, close-minded," she repeated. "And is that what you're going to call Mr. Maxwell Morris when he locks you up and throws away the key? Oh, don't open those big, gray eyes at me, honey. That's what's gonna happen when he hears about this wild scheme of yours."

The bell suddenly rang downstairs pulling both women's eyes to the well-dressed man entering the store. "Well, speak of the devil," Marion grinned. "Here's your big opportunity. You can go down there right now, and tell him how you're going to pay back all your no-good brother's debts by having a champagne and caviar cocktail party." She sat back and folded her arms as Chrystal dashed to the mirror and straightened her bangs. "Just speak loud, would you, sweetheart? I want to hear everything."

Her gaze met Marion's in the small glass as she outlined her lips in bright red lipstick then dropped the gold tube on her desk, her hand going to her skirt, smoothing the soft suede leather nervously.

Marion's expression slowly changed as she took in Chrystal's unusual primping, and the red-framed glasses she'd been twirling in her long fingers stilled then fell to the desk with a thud. Chrystal disappeared down the stairs, ignoring the black woman's arched eyebrows.

Max looked up as she came into the showroom,

and Chrystal tried to hold onto her anger. She wanted to be mad: He had no business looking for Neal. She'd thought she'd made that clear.

When his dark eyes met her pale ones, however, all she could remember was how fast her heart had beat last night when he'd put his arms around her. Her pulse was pounding the same way now, and he was at least twenty feet away from her.

Disloyalty stabbed her. How could she be attracted to a man determined to ruin her? For God's sake, he was looking for her little brother, had probably already decided to have him thrown in jail because he'd realized she'd never be able to pay the store's debts! She forced the sensual memories down and looked him straight in the eye, her voice more caustic in an effort to balance her traitorous thought. "Did you come to haul me off?"

The wince on his face told her she'd scored a direct hit. Curiously, she felt worse instead of better.

"No," he answered, his voice even, "I gave up that kind of practice several years ago. Now, I force my clients to eat Chinese food with me." He placed several blue-covered legal documents on the counter and a single rose.

She looked down at the bloom. The scarlet petals were tipped in white as though the flower had been dipped in a vat of liquid pearls. Even through her anger about Grene's call, Chrystal couldn't contain her gasp of delight as she picked it up and brought it to her nose. "My God, Max, this is the most beautiful rose I've ever seen." She couldn't resist gently fanning the soft petals against her lips. The floral kiss was as velvety as she'd imagined.

"It has a special name—'Fire and Ice.' It is gorgeous, isn't it?" He stared at her, and a sudden

intenseness darkened his face as he looked at the
petals now resting against her mouth.

His expression caused a curl of warmth to slowly
unfurl in her lower stomach, and Chrystal haltingly
lowered the flower to the counter. The powerful look
was more than she could handle. As she laid down
the rose, her eyes landed on the blue folder he'd also
brought.

"What's that?"

He cleared his throat and looked down at the document as though he had to remember himself before
he could answer. "I had a payment schedule drawn
up along with some other papers that basically outline what we already discussed. I think you should
read them."

"Certainly. Anything else?" Would he tell her
about the call to Grene, or was she going to have to
bring it up?

Max stared at her, then shook his head as if
arguing with himself. Finally he spoke. "Yes, I've
been thinking about what you said—that you thought
this whole problem was your responsibility.

"Legally, of course, you are right, but I think to
pin the whole responsibility on you is unfair. If I
could find your brother and bring him back, then we
might be able to clear you—"

"You leave Neal out of this," she hissed. "I said
I'd take care of the bills, and I will. I don't know
how, and I don't know when, but I'll handle them,
and when the time is right, I'll handle him, too."
She leaned over the glass top as if to emphasize her
point. "I know about your little phone call to the
Jeweler's Association, and I don't appreciate it.
Leave Neal out of this," she repeated.

"I want to help you, Chrystal, and Neal is the key

to this entire mess. If you'd let me go after him, we could work everything out. Why shoulder the entire burden yourself? That doesn't make any sense."

"Maybe not to you," she answered, "but from where I stand, it makes perfect sense."

"How?"

"I tried to explain that to you already," she said in a low voice.

"What I heard last night were some illogical myths you've been carrying around for ages, but nothing that made any real sense. If you don't let me find Neal, then we'll have to drag this thing out to the bitter end, punching and swinging at each other until we drop."

"What do you think bringing him back will accomplish?"

Max shook his head, his ponytail following the movement, his voice revealing his frustration. "I think he should at least be around to share the burden. You won't have a penny left, your store will be history, and your dreams dust, just because of him." He waited until she finally looked up and met his gaze. "I've got better things for us to do than argue like this, Chrystal."

Her gaze never faltered, but her knees felt weak at his look. There was no mistaking what he meant; she'd begun to want the same, but she fought to keep the conversation on a business level. "I'll cooperate but only if you leave Neal alone. I won't have him badgered."

Max snorted and looked away in disgust before facing her once more. "Good God, woman, I'm trying to help you. You make me sound like a bounty hunter. To hear you talk, you'd think I was tracking him down with my six-shooters loaded and cocked."

"Don't make fun of me, Max. I'm serious. If you try to find Neal again, you'll regret it."

No one had talked to Max in that tone of voice in a long time, and he began to understand just how much she really did love her worthless brother. Her eyes were silver chips of ice.

"I will cooperate, I will work with you, I will do whatever you want, but I will *not* let you put the responsibility for this problem on anyone but me. That is where the blame lies, and that is where the accountability will fall."

Max knew the subject was closed, whether he agreed or not. With a growing sense of frustration, he finally nodded tightly. "All right, Chrystal, if that's the way you want it."

"Yes," she said firmly, "that's the way I want it."

From the front of the store, the bell tinkled softly, and they both looked up. A small, Oriental man stood uncertainly in the doorway, and Chrystal's eyes suddenly turned friendly, making Max incongruously wish she'd look that way when he walked in.

"I've got to talk to this man. I've been waiting for him to bring me emeralds for Mrs. Meriweather. Are you finished?"

"Yes, I guess so." He searched his mind, looking for an excuse to stay a little longer, to see her tomorrow, but for the moment he was lost.

"Good." She extended her hand out over the counter, but Max wasn't about to settle for a handshake. He grabbed her fingers and pulled her over the glass. He'd thought of nothing else since he'd left her condo last night, and as she leaned over the case, he seared her mouth with his.

When he pulled away, her gray eyes were like a

lake during a thunderstorm, turbulent with confusion and denial on the surface but mysteriously dark underneath.

"Goodbye, Chrystal," and not knowing why or when, he added, "I'll see you tomorrow."

"Bye," she whispered, but he'd already turned and left, passing a well-dressed young couple coming through the door.

Marion came down the stairs to greet the customers, stopping first to hand Chrystal a Waterford vase filled with water. When she didn't move, Marion took the rose, stuck it into the vase and gently shoved Chrystal toward the Oriental man and out of the trance that had apparently rooted her to the spot.

"Mr. Kyoto," she said, struggling to recover from Max's assault, "thank you for coming. I've been waiting for you."

"Yes," he said softly. "I know. I just returned to my office this week, and as soon as I could, I came."

"Did you have a successful trip?"

"I will let you be the judge of that, Miss Chrystal."

Speaking all the way, the slight Oriental man followed Chrystal up the stairs.

"The Colombians are making life difficult for the emerald buyers, so that is why I turned to Zambia this time. I'm very pleased with the goods myself, but of course, you know your customer and what she wants."

They quickly got down to business. Several stones were shown and rejected. The fifth one the tiny man pulled from his pocket instantly caught Chrystal's eye but she tried to hide her interest.

"Not bad," she said smoothly, carefully eyeing the emerald before putting the loupe to her eye.

"What about the size?" The Oriental's voice was neutral.

"Somewhat smaller than I wanted, but it might do." A slight pause. "You have nothing else?" The briefke crinkled as she replaced the stone into the thin folded paper.

"No, that is all. The supply is tight. I confess also, my customers are not spending what they used to. They want the cheaper goods, the lighter stones. Their clients do not know the difference and do not have the money anyway."

"Well, my customer has the knowledge, but the money could be a problem. She's a serious buyer, but a tight one. How much is it?" she asked casually.

He named his figure. Chrystal's voice was even. "Mr. Kyoto, I'm a beginner at this, but I'm not stupid. Name a fair price, and I might consider the stone."

"I have a lot invested in this emerald. If I sell it for less, I will make no money."

"I find that hard to believe, Mr. Kyoto. You are too smart a buyer. Try again."

"You drive a hard bargain." He complained but named a slightly lower figure.

"Is that the best you can do?"

"Yes."

Chrystal held her breath in indecision. She knew Mrs. Meriweather would *probably* buy the stone, but if she didn't? If she didn't, Chrystal would lose her store completely because Max would never understand her one last try. If, on the other hand, the wealthy matron did buy the emerald, the profit would be very nice. Not enough to pay off Hiram but enough to . . .

Chrystal's eyes grew enormous as she considered this newest possibility. Frantically adding and subtracting in her head, she realized the sale *would* bring in enough to finance a party.

The silence stretched as she thought about all the consequences. Marion would kill her, but she'd have to stand in line because Max would be first. There was a risk, of course. If the sale didn't go through, "Cummins" would turn into "Plotsky's Hot Rocks #2."

The small office had grown warm in the bright sunshine, and Chrystal pulled at the high neck of her sweater. Mr. Kyoto stared placidly at her.

She took a deep breath and gave him her answer.

FIVE

Chrystal couldn't get thoughts of Max out of her head. During the next week, every time the bells rang over the door to the store, she'd jerk her glance to the front. When his tall form hadn't been there, she'd felt a curious mix of relief and disappointment. He managed to thoroughly confuse her every time she saw him.

Max was full of contrasts. He always brought her flowers whenever he saw her, and the blooms were always extraordinary. From a handful of French tulips to blue irises, they delighted but puzzled her. How could someone so businesslike also be such a romantic?

In addition, he knew everything about her but never discussed himself. They'd gone out several times, and she'd been impressed and entertained but each time after he'd left her on the porch, breathless from another devastating kiss, she'd realize she knew only that his parents were dead and he'd been very close to them—their only child.

She didn't seem to mind not knowing more, however, a fact she found puzzling about herself. Something about his warm dark eyes and reassuring solidness made her feel protected and cozy like sitting before a fire on a brisk California evening. Then again, something else about him made that fire flame a little higher than was comfortable, and Chrystal, always brutally honest, found herself remembering how she'd felt sitting close to him on her sofa in the darkness.

Now as she made her way to the side counter to meet Mrs. Meriweather, Chrystal forced the image of Max from her mind and tried to concentrate on the task at hand—a difficult accomplishment with Max's latest gift, a lavish bowl of gardenias, on the counter.

She had to think about her business. If Mrs. Meriweather bought the emerald whose briefke Chrystal now clutched in her hand, then the wolf might stay away from the door a little longer.

"Mrs. Meriweather, how nice to see you again. Thank you for coming down so promptly."

"Oh, Chrystal, you know I'm always anxious for a good excuse to drive over and do a little shopping. How are you, my dear?"

Chrystal smiled brightly, feeling like the biggest liar in the world. "Just fine, thanks, but where's Little Bit? Didn't you bring him today?"

The stout matron airily waved one bejeweled ring. "He's having a shampoo and a set down the street at Pierre's. Wednesday is his day for his do." As if to emphasize her connection with the tiny canine, she patted her own helmet of gray hair. "He has a standing appointment, you understand. Charles is waiting for him. When they finish, he'll bring him here."

Chrystal wondered briefly what Mrs. Meriweather's chauffeur thought about waiting for a dog while he had his weekly "do." Charles was probably accustomed to stranger tasks than that, she decided.

The Louis Quatorze chair in front of the low counter creaked as Mrs. Meriweather settled her broad frame between the delicate arms. Portions of her anatomy hung over the curved seat, her mink coat extending in a soft puddle around her as she glanced over at the flowers.

"What a gorgeous arrangement, my dear. Did Louis do those for you?"

Chrystal shook her head at the mention of Rodeo Drive's most famous floral arranger. "Oh, no. As a matter of fact, Maxwell Morris brought me those."

Mrs. Meriweather gave her a knowing look, arching one penciled eyebrow toward the ceiling. "Really?" She drew the single word out until Chrystal finally raised her eyes and smiled. "Well?"

"Well what?" Chrystal said.

"Tell me everything, darling. Everything."

From underneath the counter, Chrystal removed a black velvet display pad and deposited the briefke on top. "There's nothing to tell. We're involved professionally, that's all. The flowers were merely a courtesy."

Nervously, she opened the folded parcel, and began to speak, hoping desperately that Mrs. Meriweather would be distracted. "This emerald is from Zambia, and as you can see, the stone is very fine, indeed."

The jungle green stone looked cool and tranquil lying on the velvet pad, its polished facets reflecting the store's lights like a verdant pool. Chrystal wished she felt as calm.

"The cut is excellent, don't you think?"

Mrs. Meriweather stared at her for a long moment then finally looked down as though she knew Chrystal would say no more. "I'm certainly no expert, but the stone looks lovely. Why are the edges missing?"

With a deep sigh of relief, Chrystal ran her finger over the four facets of the rectangular shaped gem. "Emeralds are extremely fragile, Mrs. Meriweather. Angling the corners helps prevent chipping or even breakage."

"Humph. Well, that shouldn't be a problem for my daughter-in-law. Gloria never lifts a hand to do anything. I'm sure this will be the safest emerald in Los Angeles."

Chrystal hid her smile and continued. "The color is excellent, very dark yet little streaking. Sometimes, that's difficult to find. Emeralds tend to have spotty color, but this stone is very consistent."

She picked up the loupe and the stone, bringing them both to her eye, speaking as she examined the green depths. "The *jardines* are minimal. That's unusual, too."

On the other side of the counter, Mrs. Meriweather sighed. "That's so charming, don't you think? What other precious stone do you know calls its flaws 'gardens'?"

This time, Chrystal did laugh as she lowered her hand and looked at the older woman with affection. "Mrs. Meriweather, you *are* a romantic, aren't you?"

The dowager fanned her eyelashes so hard that for a moment, Chrystal could have sworn she felt a breeze. Mrs. Meriweather smiled sweetly, and placed a plump hand on her well-endowed bosom then brought her fingers to her eyes. "Arthur One always said I was a dreamer. He was the only person in the world that really understood me, that knew the real me under all this.''

"You still miss him, don't you?''

"Oh, Chrystal, he was such a wonderful man. He's been gone over a year, and my heart still flutters when I hear the front door open. I expect to see him come around the corner, holding that silly yellow rose he brought me every Tuesday for absolutely no reason at all.''

She blinked rapidly, and Chrystal felt her heart go out to the grieving woman. "Men like Arthur One just don't come along very often, Chrystal, that's why I was so glad to see Maxwell Morris in here the other day. To be honest, I'd rather hoped that, well, that he and you might be . . .''

"Oh, no, Mrs. Meriweather, believe me, you've got that one wrong. Our relationship is purely business, absolutely nothing more.''

The gray head shook regretfully. "What a shame, my dear, because that man is a dream, an absolute dream, let me tell you. Why, he reminds me so much of Arthur One, I can't believe it. Not only is he the most handsome devil I've ever met, he's generous and thoughtful as well. If I told you everything he's done for this community, you simply wouldn't believe me, why he's even—''

The front door opened with a jangle to admit Charles and Little Bit, and Chrystal breathed another sigh of relief. She had the feeling that Mrs. Meriweather could go on for quite some time about Max. Once inside, the chauffeur gently deposited the tiny dog on the carpet. With slow, measured steps, he made his way across the showroom to Mrs. Meriweather, holding his tail stiff and trying to ignore the flopping blue ribbon that hung in his eyes and hampered his self-respect.

"Oh, sweetums, don't you look precious? Did Pierre do a better job this time? Let Mommy look." She held the diminutive animal up and examined him from nose to tail while the chauffeur stood patiently by. Chrystal waited behind the counter.

"Well, he did miss a little spot back here, but we'll ignore the mistake this time." She kissed the dog and fussed a few moments more with his ribbon then deposited him on her lap. "All right," she said brusquely, returning her eyes to the emerald on the display pad. "Let's get down to business. If I don't buy this woman something soon, I'm going to regret it."

She picked up the stone and copied Chrystal by placing it on the back of her hand, twisting her fingers to catch the bright lights. "I just don't know," she murmured, "it seems a little small." She glanced up at Chrystal. "How many carats did you say the stone was?"

As she asked her question, she leaned forward, unconsciously dropping her hand until it was even with the long-suffering dog's gaze. Little Bit's black eyes snapped with avid interest, and as if he'd finally found a way of righting the affronts to his honor, his wet nose inched imperceptibly forward until it was almost touching the emerald.

Chrystal's warning was a second too late. In a flash, the dog's mouth opened, and the emerald disappeared!

Horrified, Chrystal pointed at the diminutive pet, her own mouth opening and closing uselessly. As if he sensed what he'd done, he looked up at her, pulled his lips back over his sharp, white teeth and grinned with absolute delight.

Mrs. Meriweather's eyes followed Chrystal's shaking finger to her now bare palm. "Oh, Little Bit," she gasped, "what have you done, you naughty boy?" She picked up the dog and rattled him as if the stone would come out of his ear, but he continued to smile and added a belch of satisfaction. Chrystal grabbed the edge of the counter, her life passing before her eyes.

Just then, the only thing that could make the situation worse occurred. The door opened, and Max walked in. "Well, hello, Charles," he said pleasantly to the panic-stricken driver, "how are—"

"Oh, thank God, Max, come here instantly, Little Bit just swallowed an emerald. Help me, please."

Max was too astonished to do anything but obey. He ran to Mrs. Meriweather's side.

"Don't just stand there, Charles, come over here and help, too," she gasped. "You two hold him, I'll pry his mouth open." She looked up at Chrystal, panic in her voice. "Emeralds aren't poisonous or anything, are they?"

"I, I don't think so," she stammered. Charles joined them, his mouth hanging open. "I've never known anyone that ate one before."

Max looked up at her, his expression incredulous as he took the back end of the wiggling dog from Mrs. Meriweather's hands. Charles got the end with teeth. Little Bit promptly delivered an exasperated bite to the black-gloved hands.

"Little Bit," Mrs. Meriweather pleaded, "calm down, darling, and let Mommie look." Her eyes shot to Charles's. "Hold him tight, you silly man," she instructed. "How can I look in his mouth if he's twisting around like that?"

Chrystal stood helpless behind the counter. Her eyes closed briefly, and black dots swam behind her lids. She heard the wet snap of the dog's mouth as he clicked his teeth. Mrs. Meriweather's voice came from a far away distance.

"Little Bit, you've been a bad baby, bad."

Chrystal opened her eyes. The little dog was stretched between Max and Charles, and as the magic word reached his hairy ears, he suddenly stopped his struggles and held his mouth open with resignation. Mrs. Meriweather peered inside then shook her head and stared him down. He hung his head, the enormity of his transgression beginning to become apparent as Max gently relinquished his end to Charles. The grayhaired matron continued her tirade.

"Bad, do you hear me? Bad. I cannot believe you ate that emerald. Really—what am I going to do about this?"

He slowly lifted his head and looked at her with the most pitiful expression Chrystal had ever encountered, human or otherwise. With a tiny whine of apology, he dropped his eyes and peeked out at her from under the now-untied blue ribbon.

Mrs. Meriweather raised an imperious hand and waved towards the door. "Take him away, Charles. Wait in the car."

The dog tried one last whimper, but Mrs. Meriweather turned her back on him, facing the jewelry counter once more. As Charles unceremoniously hauled him away, Chrystal could have sworn the now extremely valuable dog wore a very pleased look. Chrystal wanted to scream and run after the man and pet, but she stayed behind the counter and faced Mrs.

Meriweather instead. Silently, Max stood to one side, clearly bewildered, and waiting to hear more.

"Well, Chrystal, I don't know what to say except exactly how much did that emerald cost?"

Chrystal felt her knees buckle, but she held on to the counter and named the figure. Mrs. Meriweather's sigh was only slightly exasperated. "He is a naughty little thing, isn't he?"

"Yes," Chrystal swallowed hard. Surely Mrs. Meriweather would pay her now, *wouldn't she?*

The matron's thoughtful look sent shivers of dread down Chrystal's stiff spine. "When it comes out, uh, well, I mean, when I have the stone in my hands again, I'll return and we may resume our discussion. I'd like to examine the cut a little closer before I decide."

Chrystal nodded mutely, her shock temporarily paralyzing her tongue. There was nothing she could do. If she was obnoxious about the situation, Mrs. Meriweather would be less inclined than ever to buy the emerald. *The customer is always right—right?* Chrystal felt a hysterical giggle well up between her breasts. Even if their pets ate the merchandise? she wondered wildly. Finally, she found her voice. "How long do you think . . ."

"Tonight is his steak night, so it shouldn't be long. A day or so at the most." She rose and gathered her mink coat, turning to go. As she reached the front door, she paused, a smile wreathing her broad face. "I must say, this does have a bit of humor, doesn't it?"

"Humor?" Chrystal squeaked.

"Yes, I mean, considering why I was buying the stone and who would be wearing it." She started to giggle and ended up laughing uproariously, gasping to catch her breath as she held on to the open door. "Oh, my word, if Gloria ever found out she might be wearing Little Bit's leftovers, she'd die. She'd just die." The door swung open and closed, laughter trailing outside into the sunshine.

Chrystal collapsed into the chair at her side as Max took Mrs. Meriweather's now vacant seat. She wanted to crawl under the nearest counter and howl, but knowing that was somewhat undignified, she settled for dropping her face into her hands and groaning.

"What in the hell was all that about, Chrystal?"

She took a deep breath behind the protection of her fingers then finally raised her resigned eyes to his face. "That," she said dramatically, "was my Waterloo."

To her amazement, he grinned broadly. "Well, thank God."

She raised her eyebrows at his reaction. A smile was definitely not what she'd been expecting.

"I thought I was the worst thing that had happened to you lately. I'm happy to know I've been jostled out of first place, but I'm slightly confused—"

Ten minutes later, he was no longer smiling and the easy slouch had fled as he sat up straight in the chair and gripped the polished arms. "Are you telling me that was *your* emerald? I thought it was hers!"

Chrystal shook her head. "I was showing it to her—she hadn't purchased the stone—yet."

"I just assumed she had brought it in here for you to look at . . ." Max shot a look over his shoulder as if he'd like to chase Mrs. Meriweather's limo down Rodeo Drive and stop her, but it was too late. He turned back to face Chrystal, his expression thunderous. "Let me get this straight. You're planning a party, and you were going to pay for it by selling an emerald, but the dog ate it. He ate a fifty thousand dollar emerald." Max paused, his face turning red. "He ate a fifty thousand dollar emerald, *that wasn't even paid for,* and you let him walk out of here?"

"What else could I do? Keep the dog hostage? You know how crazy Mrs. Meriweather is about Little Bit. She'd stay a hostage herself before she'd let me keep him." She paused just a second. "Actually, I don't think I'd *want* that dog around. I couldn't afford to feed him." For a second she frowned, then a short, hysterical laugh escaped as she thought about what she'd just said.

"Well, why didn't you make her pay for the stone?"

"Max," Chrystal protested, her nervous giggles disappearing, "I can't do that. Mrs. Meriweather is a good client. If I offend her, I might as well kiss my party off."

Unexpectedly, he stood up, pushing the chair almost over. "That's another thing, Chrystal. I can't actually believe you think you're going to have a party for four hundred people and serve them champagne and caviar."

"There's no 'thinking' about it, Max. I'm going to have that party, it's my last chance."

"Last chance? It's your last chance, all right. The last chance you'll have to get thrown in jail." He gripped the back of the chair, his knuckles turning white. "Do I need to remind you that you owe substantial amounts of money to various businesses in this city? Excuse me, but I do not understand how having a party will help you pay those debts."

"I already explained, Max. I've got a special supplier from New York coming. Everyone will go wild over her pieces, and I'll make more than enough to pay you off.''

"Right," he said sarcastically. "Just like you made money off Mrs. Meriweather to pay for the party."

Chrystal stood up, her movement sending her own chair rocking dangerously near the glass case. "How could I know the damned dog would eat the emerald? My plan was, *is*," she corrected herself, "a good one and when Mrs. Meriweather buys that stone, I'll have plenty of money for the party."

"And if no one comes?"

"They'll come, I know they will."

"That's crazy, Chrystal," he sputtered, his anger finally out of control. "I'm beginning to think Neal's not the only irresponsible one around here. Maybe your father knew something when he said you couldn't run the business."

She gasped, his accusation hanging between them like a block of ice, freezing her into speechlessness. How dare he accuse her, *her*, of irresponsibility? Her lips moved, but she was so angry, the words wouldn't come out.

More painful than the anger, however, was the sudden sting of self-doubt Max's words reactivated. What *would* her father say? Was this any way to run a business? She swallowed hard, her throat burning with the effort. How *could* she justify her actions?

He continued to shake his head, the black ponytail swinging with each movement. "I'm sorry, Chrystal, but you've obviously been working too hard. Your judgment on this one is way off. If you've made any plans for that party, you'll just have to cancel them. I can't allow it."

"You, you can't what?"

He looked at her as if she were a small child. "I said I will not allow you to spend the funds for a party. If Mrs. Meriweather comes through and buys that emerald, then you must apply the proceeds to your debts. A party is out of the question."

"You can't tell me what to do."

"I'm afraid I can, in this case."

She raised her hand and sharply poked one long pink fingernail into Max's chest. "You can't stop me. I still own Cummins and the day-to-day operations are under my control. If I want to have a party, then I can have a party. As long as I make your payment schedule, then I can do whatever I damn well please."

When Max grabbed her hand in his, she automatically pulled back but he tightened his grip and pulled her inextricably towards him. She was forced to steady herself by grabbing his shoulder with her free hand. His voice was a low growl. "And do you understand what happens if you don't make those payments?"

Her heart was beating so fast, Chrystal was sure Max could hear the thumping. "Yes," she said bravely, "I'll lose the store to Hiram."

Max's smile was grim. "And you're willing to run the chance? To gamble everything on one turn of the wheel?"

Her vision was filled with his face, the harsh angles shadowed by the soft lights above as his words took on a more subtle meaning. Her fingers tightened on his jacket, her eyes bored into his.

"Yes," she whispered, "I think it's time to gamble."

*　　*　　*

Chrystal looked down at the slip of paper in her hand then back up at the dilapidated house. Could Marion have made a mistake? Surely, a legal clinic wouldn't look so run down, so unkempt?

She stood uncertainly on the sidewalk then moved closer. At one end of the wide covered porch, a Latino teenager suffered his mother's harangue, delivered in scathing Spanish, while at the other end, two small children played in the dust near the dying rosebushes. A fat yellow cat primped in the sunlight at the top of the broken down handrail where Chrystal's hand now rested. The small sign to the right of the door reassured her that the Los Angeles Legal Assistance Coalition (LALAC) did indeed reside inside.

Still not sure she was doing the right thing, Chrystal stopped and turned once more to look at the surroundings. Across the street, an equally run-down house stood forlornly, two disassembled cars parked on the brown grass out front. At least a half-dozen children ran around the engine parts and jumped on the car seats scattered in the yard like upholstered boulders. Why weren't they in school?

Surely the people that came here had more important concerns than whether or not their business was successful, especially a jewelry store, but she'd been desperate since Mrs. Meriweather's visit. Thanks to Little Bit, Chrystal felt like her whole life was going down the drain. Max knowing her plans about the party put added pressure on her. When Marion had mentioned the clinic again, Chrystal had decided the time had come to get a second opinion.

She glanced through the window to the offices inside. The attorneys looked like high school kids, for God's sake. The girl in the corner was surely wearing her mother's business suit, and the boy in the white short-sleeved shirt had an earring! How could she pit them against Max? He had suits more expensive than this house.

In her head, thoughts of Neal buzzed around like the flies that were sharing the front porch with her. She inattentively swatted at them and heard the echo of Max's words—the echo she'd been unable to silence since he'd spoken.

"You've never let him grow up . . . big sister to protect him . . . always fought his battles for him." Was this true? When they were children and her father had made her responsible for her brother, she'd done the best she could. Obviously, that hadn't been good enough. But Max's words had triggered another reaction, a feeling she couldn't release. Had she done *too* good of a job?

The creaking screen door jarred her out of her dilemma. An elderly lady and the young man with an earring came out this time. He solicitously cradled her elbow in one large hand then helped her down the steps. When they reached the sidewalk, he matched her painful shuffle, and they progressed at an agonizing pace to the bus stop on the corner. In a few seconds, the long, diesel-belching vehicle arrived, and he supported her as she tortuously climbed aboard. Chrystal watched him pay the woman's fare, settle her into a seat, then dash off the bus just before the vehicle roared off in a cloud of gritty dust.

He ran back to the porch where Chrystal waited and bounded up the steps in one jump, landing right before her with a big smile. The small gold loop in his ear lobe gave his face a rakish look, contradicting his otherwise conservative appearance, but the wrin-

kles that formed when he smiled told Chrystal he
was a little older than she'd first thought.

"Hi. Are you waiting for someone?" he said in a
friendly voice.

"Not really, but I . . ." She didn't quite know
how to explain and her words dwindled off.

"Need some help?" he supplied.

She nodded silently.

"Well, that's what we're here for. Come on in,
we'll talk."

Chrystal rose and went through the open door he
held for her. After the bright light outside, her eyes
adjusted slowly to the dim interiors. A blast of hot
air from the ceiling fan above hit her. No wonder he
didn't wear a suit, she realized guiltily, the house
wasn't air conditioned.

He led her to the back and his office, which had
obviously been the dining room of the home. A lop-
sided chandelier hung over his desk and built-in corner hutches served as bookcases. He plopped into a
chair on one side of the dining table and indicated
she take the one on the other side.

"I'm Jeff McDonald," he said, extending his
hand. "How can I help you, Miss—?"

"Cummins, Chrystal Cummins. Nice to meet you,
Jeff. I have a business situation that I need some
help with."

The chair he'd been tilting back on two legs came
forward in a crash as she introduced herself, and
Chrystal knew instantly that she'd been right. Her
problem was not the kind of thing this clinic would
want to handle.

"Chrystal Cummins?" he repeated her name as if
he recognized it, his voice cracking slightly.

She frowned then answered. "Yes, that's right. I

wouldn't have come except I was desperate, and a friend of mine thought you might help.''

"A friend of yours?'' he repeated.

Chrystal was beginning to wonder if she even wanted Jeff McDonald's help—all he seemed capable of doing was repeating her words. "Yes, Marion Hall, a woman who works for me. She had another friend you helped with a rent situation so I thought . . .''

He nodded and his hand crept up to the gold loop which he twisted nervously. "And do you have a rent problem?'' he asked almost hopefully.

"No,'' Chrystal said, her mystification growing. "A business one. I bought a store from my brother without knowing that he owed a lot of money. Now I've been threatened—''

"Threatened?''

"Yes,'' she said, trying to hide her exasperation at his parrotlike behavior, "threatened by a hot-shot LA attorney who wants to take over my store for his client. You probably know him, Maxwell Morris.''

"Yes,'' he cleared his throat quickly. "I do know Mr. Morris.''

At least this time he didn't mock her words, but what he finally did say aggravated her even more. She hadn't even presented her case, and Max's name had already intimidated him. With a discouraged sigh, Chrystal reached into her briefcase and removed the legal papers Max had given her last week.

"I'm sure you can make more sense of these than I can,'' she said, handing him one of the thicker documents with a feeling of hopelessness.

He adjusted his tortoise shell glasses and quickly scanned the papers that Chrystal had poured over for days.

The hot silence extended as he continued to read, and Chrystal brushed at her bangs, the dust, the heat, the sweltering humidity beginning to get to her, along with her growing sense of frustration. "Maxwell Morris is a pretty awesome opponent. I'd understand if you didn't want to fight him."

The young attorney leaned back and put his hands behind his head, smiling greatly. "Are you kidding? I'd love to take Max on. The question is could you gain anything in the deal?"

Chrystal blinked and sat back down. "He doesn't scare you?"

Jeff laughed this time when he repeated her words. "Scare me? Hell, no. He's got a few more years on me, but he doesn't frighten me a bit. I'd get a kick out of arguing against him. But there's absolutely no reason for this to go to court."

The faint glimmer of hope, the first she'd had, was instantly extinguished. He tapped the blue papers. "I see a few minor points I'd contest, but frankly, Ms. Cummins, this proposal is more than fair to both parties. If you tried to fight the offer, you'd only lose more money." The hard slats of the dining room chair bit into her back as she slumped against the unrelenting wood. "If you've got the time, however, I'd be happy to ask him my questions. Won't take but a minute," he continued cheerily.

Without waiting for an answer, he picked up the papers and headed for the door. "Just sit tight, I'll see if he's busy."

The phone on his desk must be out of order, she thought distractedly, standing and moving to the window on her right. Her shoulders slumped dejectedly, and she pressed her forehead against the glass, closing her eyes.

She didn't hear the door open, and he was grateful for the moment. Her slim figure was outlined by the sunshine pouring through the glass and past the thin material of her simple white skirt and blouse, and the surge of desire Max felt every time he'd seen her from the very first hit him anew. She looked so fragile, but with every passing day, he saw more and more of her strength.

"Chrystal?" he said tentatively, not sure how she would react to his presence in a place she'd come to for help.

At the sound of his voice, she swirled, instantly straightening her spine. Her gray eyes were huge. "What are you doing here?" she cried. "Where's Jeff? I thought he meant he was going to call you, I didn't think—"

Max held up his hand for silence. "This is my clinic, Chrystal. I sponsor all the law students here." Her look of disbelief hurt. "What's wrong?" he asked ruefully. "Don't you think I'm capable of helping people who can't pay?"

"No, I," she stuttered, "I just wasn't expecting you, that's all." She waved her hand, indicating the tiny office. "You've never said anything about this. I thought, well, guess I thought you had a fancy office somewhere."

"I do, but I spend my free time here." He shut the door behind him and walked to the dining table where he casually rested one hip against the wooden edge. He let his eyes slide over her. "I'm glad to see you."

She didn't meet his stare. "I thought it might be smart to get another opinion."

"It is. Frankly, I'm relieved to see you here."

She jerked her head up. "Why?"

"I think it's always good to have more than one opinion. Besides, it wouldn't be fair for me to be the sole attorney in this case—"

"Why?" This time the word was whispered as though she already knew the answer but wanted to ask him anyway.

"Why do you think?"

She shook her head and remained silent. He was tempted to show her instead of tell her, but he forced himself to stay still, knowing that once he felt her skin beneath his fingers, her mouth under his, he wouldn't be able to stop. He cleared his throat. "In divorce cases, parties frequently share attorneys to cut down on costs. It's more unusual in a situation like this, but frankly, I didn't have a problem with it until, well . . ."

"Until Hiram asked?" she guessed.

He acknowledged her speculation with a smile. "You got it."

"So what are you going to do? Tell me to find another attorney?"

"No. Hiram and I worked out a deal—I traded my fee for something he needed to do anyway. That way I'm not really representing either of you."

Her forehead wrinkled. "But what about your money—"

He shook his head. "It's okay. I make enough off Hiram in other ways. Hell, the charges on his divorces alone keep this clinic going."

This finally brought a smile to her mouth. "Hiram—a philanthropist? That's a real oxymoron." She looked around the clinic once more. "Almost as unexpected as—" she stopped suddenly, her face turning pink with embarrassment.

Even before she'd said a word, Max had known

what she was thinking, and his amusement fled. He wanted her to see him as he really was—not as he appeared to be. "Me helping other people? I used to be a public defender, Chrystal. Before I started my private practice here in LA, I worked in San Diego defending the kind of people who lived in neighborhoods a helluva lot worse than this one."

The disbelief on her face lightened his mood and he grinned once more. "What can't you believe? That I would do that kind of work, or that there are worse neighborhoods?"

She smiled faintly. "Both, I guess."

His own grin faded, and he rose and crossed the dusty floor to look out the window where she stood. "Believe it. I had cases down there I'll never be able to get out of my mind."

Seeing her here reminded him too much of another time and another woman he'd tried to help. The memories flooded him, swamped him, and he couldn't stop the wave.

He shook his head, trying to dislodge the images from his mind and the long hair sticking to his hot, sweaty neck, but he failed on both accounts. "There was one woman, Tia Sanchez—" he stopped and pointed to the blue lapis on his finger. "She's the one who gave me this ring. In fact, it'd been her father's."

He looked at Chrystal, pleading with his eyes for her to understand because suddenly he needed her to appreciate his past, to understand him. "You remind me of her, I guess, something about your dignity, your strength. She lived with this guy who beat her. I tried to get her to leave him, but she wouldn't. They had a young child together, and Tia felt he needed a father, even a worthless one."

The bitterness tasted like copper in his mouth, and even though years had passed, Max still felt the acrid sting of regret. "One night, he took a knife and stabbed them both, killed them." He swallowed hard. "I had to defend him, and I did a good job." He deliberately made his voice flat and neutral, trying to hide the guilt that still tormented him on lonely mornings at 3 A.M.. "I got the bastard off, and the following year, he killed another woman.

"I stuck around for a while longer. There was always someone who needed help. If their boss accused them of stealing, I'd bail them out. If the landlord wouldn't pay his utilities, I'd see that they had water." His voice cracked, but he continued. "Finally, I couldn't take the grief any longer. That's when I left San Diego and came to LA."

He stared out the glass. "I started the clinic here, about a year ago, I guess." Her eyes were shining as he looked down at her, and Max knew suddenly that he'd done the right thing in telling her. Chrystal moved closer and put her hand on his trembling arm.

Seeking the comfort he'd denied himself for so long, he fit his arms around her slender body and tightened them. She murmured softly and patted his back, pulling the misery from him like a sponge. As Max released the hurt he'd lived with for so long, his senses flooded with the immediacy of the situation, and instantly Chrystal's soft curves and sustaining touch aroused him. He found himself searching for more, wanting more.

With the open palms of his hands, he cradled her cheeks, lifting her face to his, seeking her lips. She automatically closed her eyes, and raised her face to his, tightening her arms about his waist. Bending down to meet her mouth with his, he pulled her closer.

His kiss was harsh, and Chrystal knew he was trying to erase the bitterness his memories had aroused, but even that knowledge didn't stop her body from responding. She molded against him as he claimed her lips with his. His chest was hard against her own, and her breasts flattened then grew warm with desire as he continued to pull her into his heat.

All thought of business fled, banished by his opening mouth and probing tongue. His passion overpowered her, and she felt her knees turn even weaker as his hands left her face to slide down the curve of her back.

She murmured and thought about telling him to stop but she couldn't. She'd already made the decision to take a chance on him, and Chrystal was too honest to deny the waves of pleasure washing through her. When the door to the office suddenly opened, and Max lifted his dark head, the loss that she felt stabbed her deeply.

He whirled, his broad back giving her the privacy to recover, while he addressed the startled young attorney waiting awkwardly by the door. "What is it, McDonald?" he barked.

"I, uh, I have those changes ready we discussed. I thought Ms. Cummins might want to go over them."

"Fine, fine," Max said, smoothing one hand over his head to the ponytail at his neck, "leave them, and I'll explain them to her." A small silence ensued, then Chrystal heard Jeff's hesitant voice.

"I thought I'd do that myself, if you don't mind, Max. After all, she did come here for help, and I feel somewhat responsible.'' He cleared his throat, his voice apologetic. ''I'm sure you understand.''

''Yes,'' Max said, his own tones ironic, ''I understand, Jeff.'' He faced Chrystal, his rueful smile causing a curious hunger in the pit of her stomach. ''After your attorney explains the changes to you, I'd like to see you. Be ready at eight.''

She nodded silently, too confused to do anything else, then he leaned closer and spoke into her ear. ''Wear something special.''

He turned and left Chrystal with a pounding heart and racing pulse to face the puzzled Jeff. All she could do was shrug her shoulders. How could she explain? She didn't understand herself.

SIX

Trying not to glance again at her watch, Chrystal stood restlessly beside the window in her living room. Max would be here any minute to pick her up. The last time she'd felt this mixture of dread and excitement while waiting for an escort was her senior prom.

Her date that night had been Perry Townsend, a friend of Neal's. She'd always wondered if her brother had bribed the football player to take her out, but she'd never asked. She didn't really want to know.

In a way, she felt the same about Max. Why did he find her attractive? She knew what she liked about him; he was the kind of man she'd always wanted, sophisticated yet kind, smooth but sincere, sexy beyond belief. From that first day when he'd walked into the store, she'd been attracted to him, and the struggle to ignore that pull was almost more than she could bear.

So why did she try? Chrystal grimaced and shook

her head as if answering her own unspoken question. A relationship with an attorney who was suing her just didn't seem right, and besides, the business took all her energies right now. She didn't have time for Max and his flowers, Max and his devastating kisses, Max and his anything else.

The door bell interrupted her thoughts and sent her pulse pounding. She smoothed her black silk dress and strode to the entry. Max would have his one evening; then, she resolved, this relationship would turn professional again.

That decision fled, along with her breath, when she opened the door. He wore a custom made tuxedo as casually as some men wear blue jeans, and his radiant self-confidence almost overpowered her as he stepped inside.

He brushed his lips across her cheek then handed her an exquisite lily. She shook her head and laughed as she took it.

"You're going to spoil me, you know. You can't keep bringing me these gorgeous flowers." There were several blooms on the single stem but the center one was at least seven inches in diameter. They were pure white and the fragrance that rose to meet her could only be described as sensual.

"This is a Casa Blanca Lily." Enclosing her fingers with his own, he brought the flower and her hand to his face, breathing deeply. "Their perfume reminds me of you—strong yet so feminine." Immediately, he turned her hand over and exposed her palm. Before she could react, he kissed the tender center and smiled.

Dreamlike, Chrystal floated to the kitchen, put the bloom into a vase then turned and went back to the front door where Max was waiting. They stepped outside to the black limo waiting at the curb. She'd seen the easy wealth flowing in and out of the store; women who thought nothing of buying themselves a sapphire necklace to chase the blues, men who purchased three pairs of diamond earrings when they came in—one for their mother, one for their wife, one for their mistress, but even in that kind of world, Mercedes limos were rare. Climbing into the leather interior, she felt her excitement grow, and a small thrill of delight over the pure luxury of the situation chased down her spine. She felt like Cinderella.

With a deep purr, the limo pulled away, and Chrystal turned to Max, her hand caressing the smoothness of the seats. "This is a beautiful car, Max."

"Thanks. I felt pretty uncomfortable at first, but my client insisted. He said if I turned the car down, he'd sue me."

"A client gave you this?" Her voice rose in shock.

"Yes, I'm afraid so. It was a nasty divorce case, and he was so grateful that I'd saved his company from his wife's clutches that he insisted on giving me the car. He said it was all he had left, and I ought to have it." He shrugged and leaned over to the built-in bar in front of them. "Would you like a drink?"

Chrystal nodded. "Perrier would be fine." She watched his long fingers twist open the bottle cap then reach for the ice tongs and crystal tumbler.

"Here," he said, handing her the glass. "I have a toast." She raised her eyebrows as he gently touched the rim of his tumbler to hers. "To Cummins and success."

His salute was the last thing she would have

expected, but Chrystal smiled in genuine delight. Was he beginning to understand what her store meant to her?

As if he'd read her mind, his next words confirmed her thoughts. "We're going to talk business on the way to the restaurant, but after we arrive, I absolutely forbid any other mention of work. All right? This is my evening, and you have to play by my rules."

She went along, intrigued. "Okay. You're the boss."

"Right," he said in mock seriousness, "now, here's the deal. I want to get something straight about this party you're having."

Chrystal brought her glass up to her suddenly dry lips. She didn't want to start the evening with a fight, but she would if he forced her. Mrs. Meriweather had returned, check in hand, and Chrystal had immediately started planning the party.

"The way I see it, you've got everything already in motion. Right?"

She nodded.

"The invitations are sent, the food's been ordered. I assume you've already arranged for your New York dealer to come."

"That's correct. To cancel now would be extremely expensive, and I've—"

"Whoa, stop right there. I didn't say anything about canceling."

Her forehead knit in the dim light of the back seat. "Isn't that what you're working up to? I just assumed . . ."

He tapped a nail on the rim of the crystal tumbler then looked at her. "That impression is exactly what

I want to apologize for. The store is yours, and I was wrong to give you a hard time about the party.''

Chrystal raised her glass once more. This was not at all what she'd expected.

He went on. "I've been thinking about what you said, the fact that Mrs. Meriweather is helping you by calling her friends and everything.'' He looked up at her, his dark face shadowed in the corner of the car. "I'd like to do the same, if you'll let me.''

Chrystal swallowed her sparkling water quickly, then tried not to cough. "You, you want to help with the party?''

"Yes.''

The silence built as she thought about his offer. Max was a powerful, well-known figure in Los Angeles; he could bring in a lot of rich people. On the other hand, her natural tendencies made her suspicious of his motives.

"Max, I'm sorry, but I don't think I understand. When I told you about the party, you called me irresponsible. Now you want to help? I find it hard to believe that just because Mrs. Meriweather is helping, you decided to jump on the bandwagon.''

He leaned closer, and his face came out of the shadows. "I don't follow the pack, Chrystal. Elizabeth Meriweather is a shrewd woman, and anything she'd back is sure to be a success, but that's not why I changed my mind. I changed my mind because I thought about what you're trying to do and realized you'd made a good decision, a sound move.''

As his simple words of praise soaked in, Chrystal's pride began to swell. No one had ever acknowledged her business skills before, and the sudden lift she felt was almost euphoric. She hadn't realized until this moment how much she'd wanted Max's approval.

"I'm, I'm glad you feel this way," she said, stumbling over the words. "I'd be delighted for you to help."

When she heard his soft expulsion of breath, she suddenly realized he'd wanted her respect as much as she'd wanted his, and this new knowledge endeared him to her more than any sweet words would have done.

"Great," he said, pulling a piece of paper from his breast pocket and handing it to her. "Here's a list of my polo club members and some of my friends I think would come. I've called a few of them already, and they seemed intrigued by the idea."

She laughed, not surprised that he'd already drawn up the roster, confident of her assent. Quickly, she glanced at it. The roll included names the whole world would recognize. Folding the list once, she slipped it into her bag then looked up at him. "You didn't have to do this," she said softly.

He took her glass and placed the tumbler beside his own on the small table before them then lifted a hand to her cheek, cupping her jaw. His palm was warm against her skin, and an almost electric sensation passed through her at his touch. "I know, but I wanted to," he said and dropped his voice even lower. "And I'd like to do a lot more, if you'll let me, Chrystal. From the very beginning, I told you I was on your side, but you didn't believe me."

She stared into his black eyes, mesmerized by his liquid voice and impelling words. Hesitant to acknowledge what he was saying but compelled to be honest, she finally nodded her head, dropping her gaze in her lap. "I know," she whispered, "but . . ."

"But what?" he questioned. "Why didn't you believe me?" He moved his fingers beneath her chin and lifted her face to his. "I can understand your initial reservations, but now, well, things have changed, haven't they?"

She captured his hand in hers and brought their entangled fingers to her lap, staring at him. "Yes, they have. You don't understand, though. No one has ever helped me before, Max. After my mother died, I was on my own."

His face softened instantly and his hand tightened on hers. "I felt the same way after my father passed away."

She felt his stare on the side of her face as he continued. "I thought then that if I had a brother or sister, they'd be a comfort."

His words evoked a wistful shake to her head. "My brother couldn't even take care of himself, much less help me." She sighed and shook her head. "I'd have to admit, though, that it would have been awfully lonely without him. But Dad was still there, and he didn't care." She shook her head again. "I've gotten where I am today because of hard work and perseverance, not by clinging to someone else's coattails."

"Accepting help is not 'clinging to coattails,' Chrystal."

She tried not to shiver. Even discussing this made her feel vulnerable and exposed. "I know that," she said quietly, "but I was taught to be self-reliant, and in my heart of hearts, I grew up believing it was a sign of weakness to get help."

He sighed. "I have a hard time understanding how

a little kid can feel that way, but my parents were always there for me when I needed them. I can argue with one thing, though.''

"Okay, what's that?"

"You aren't a child anymore, Chrystal. You're a grown woman, and you obviously understand yourself quite well. Why do you still believe you can't accept help?"

"I don't think I do believe that anymore, but I didn't realize it till now. Maybe you changed my mind." The wonder in her voice revealed her surprise as she looked at Max, the orange glow of the streetlight flooding the back seat. The car had stopped.

He grinned broadly. "Well, I'm glad we had this little discussion then. Shall we get on with our evening?"

Her slight form was warm and soft in his arms, and Max gave into the urge to pull her closer. She didn't protest, and he felt a spark of hope.

The dim club wrapped dark fingers of smoke and perfume around them, entwining them with ambiance. As they danced, Max knew they looked like lovers—the lovers he planned for them to become.

His lips brushed her ear, and he wanted to tell her how he felt, but instead he kept quiet, afraid to break the silence. Holding her in his arms was like feeding a wild deer; he couldn't believe she was this close, and he didn't want to scare her off with any sudden moves.

Surprisingly, she moved closer to him. The silk of her dress felt slippery beneath his hands and through the material, the warmth of her back radiated to his palm. Max wished away even the thin barrier, imagining how the texture of her skin would feel against his. Instinctively, he knew she would feel softer than the silk now beneath his touch, fine and smooth.

As the music pulled them into a magic sense of isolation, Max tightened his arms around her and enjoyed the powerful sensations that were rocking him. He'd never felt this way about a woman, and now that he'd managed to convince her to accept his help, maybe he could also make her see that what they had between them was something they shouldn't let slip away.

When the sensuous music stopped and Chrystal pulled from his arms, Max felt an instant loss. He draped his arm casually around her shoulders as they walked slowly back to their table. As long as he could touch her, he felt whole, complete. He wondered if she felt the same way.

Max held back the curtains partially covering the booth as Chrystal slid across the curved seat. Before following her, he flicked his eyes toward the waiter and signaled for another bottle of champagne. She protested as the waiter whisked away the empty and replaced the bottle with another. "Max, we've already had one. That's enough, really."

As the waiter presented the Dom Perignon then removed the cork, Max smiled and nodded, ignoring Chrystal's objection until the black-clad man had disappeared. "I thought I was in charge of this evening. It was one of the rules, remember?"

She grinned. "Sorry, I forgot, but those are your rules. I don't have to live by them."

"Oh, yes, you do. That's another rule—you have to follow all my rules. You can't do anything but be agreeable, otherwise you have to forfeit." Between his thumb and forefinger, Max twisted a strand of her hair, the ebony curl incredibly soft to his touch.

In the darkness, she arched her eyebrows. "Forfeit? Forfeit what?"

"Whatever I want," he said, his voice deliberately low. "I'm making the rules. Your sacrifice can be anything I want."

"This sounds serious," she said, the light in her gray eyes dispelling her words. "Sacrifice brings to mind young virgins thrown to the volcano. I don't think I want that."

He frowned, a mock look of horror. "Oh, heavens, no. That's too much of a waste. If we sacrifice someone's life, we don't use virgins." He tried to grin diabolically. "We have other uses for our virgins."

"I'm sure you do."

"I'm glad you understand," he said silkily, secretly delighted with this new playful side of Chrystal he hadn't seen before. "Then we can move on to our other, more creative penances."

Her lips parted. She sipped the champagne, her eyes huge over the crystal rim. "And they are?"

He dropped the strand of hair and traced a finger down her neck to the warm curve of her shoulder. "Well, you've already been forced to endure one."

"And I didn't know it?"

"Yes, eating Chinese takeout food at your kitchen table is the first torture, you see. No one should ever have to do that."

"If that's a sacrifice, then I'm in trouble. I thought the dumplings were great."

"Oh, I wasn't talking about the food."

"What then?"

"Eating at the table," he whispered. "Don't you know Chinese takeout is always supposed to be eaten in bed?"

Her eyes didn't falter from his. "No, I didn't know that. I might not qualify for the virgin sacrifice, but I'm not exactly in your league."

He threw back his head and laughed, delighted. "And just what is my 'league'?"

She waved a vague hand. "All this, the smokey bar, the cold champagne, a booth with curtains. I've never been in a place like this before, and you look awfully comfortable. I figured you came here often."

He sipped his drink slowly. "Actually, I haven't dated much since my divorce. My ex-wife frightened me into staying home."

"I can't imagine anyone scaring you."

"I can see you don't really know me very well, either that or you don't know my ex."

Chrystal laughed. "Come on. She couldn't have been that bad."

Max's expression turned serious. "You're right. Veronica was actually a decent person when we met, but somewhere down the line, she got confused. You know the expression 'Charity starts at home'? Well, she never heard it. She was so busy taking care of every charity organization that came down the pike that she forgot about me and our marriage."

His dark eyes turned soft. "The funny thing is, that's what attracted me to her, at first. I was a hot-shot public defender, and she was out to save the world." He paused, his regrets obvious.

Chrystal felt a moment's flash of jealousy. What kind of woman would leave a man who could still look like that about her, five years and one divorce later?

He shook his head slightly as if to dispel his disappointments. "She's gone on to bigger and better things, now."

"So have you."

His smile sent her heart into overtime, and he moved closer to her on the banquette, his long, muscular thigh burning against her leg. "That's true," he admitted. "I did that when I met you."

Chrystal felt her face grow warm, with embarrassment over his flattery or desire from his touch, she didn't know. In an attempt to cover her discomfort, she let her glance search the room while her mind searched for a new topic of conversation. Finally, under his unrelenting gaze, she spoke. "Do you bring all your potential victims to swanky places like this?"

"God, you make me sound like a vampire instead of an attorney."

"One and the same?"

He frowned, a mock fierceness, his own mood lightening again. "Please, I thought I said no business, remember?"

She bit her lip and feigned distress, bringing a hand to her throat. "Oh, no, I broke another rule, didn't I?"

"That's right. You're going to be in deep trouble when we add all these up. In fact, you might not have anything left, by the end of the evening. Those forfeits can get pretty steep."

"In that case, I better start working some of them off." She nodded toward the floor. "Would another dance help?"

"Tremendously."

When the music stopped, they didn't part. The rest of the evening passed in a blur for Max. A kaleidoscope of sensations he knew he'd never forget. The smell of her warm skin, the touch of her hand around his neck, the sound of her whispers in his ear, and finally, on the steps of her door, the taste of champagne from her lips.

"Let me come in," he said, lifting his head from their kiss. "I don't want the evening to end this way." She said nothing, but he sensed her hesitation. "Why not, Chrystal? We have something special, can't you feel it? I can."

"Yes," she whispered, "but . . ."

"But what?"

She shook her head, drawing a breath so deep he could feel her shoulders move. "I need some time to think."

"That's the worst thing you can do, Chrystal. Don't think, just feel."

"I can't," she cried. "I'm not that kind of person. I don't just act, I have to decide before I do something."

"Let me decide for you," he pressed. "You know we're right for each other. What's left to think about?"

She continued to shake her head then laid a finger against his lips. "Don't, Max. Don't push me. When the time is right, it'll happen. Right now, there are too many issues between us. When they're settled—"

An angry protest formed and died before he could give it voice. He knew, as sure as he'd known anything in his life, that they were right for each other, and if it took him the rest of his days to convince her, he'd spend them trying. "All right," he said hoarsely, "I'll give you as much time as you want, but remember one thing. When I call in my markers, you're mine."

"Plan for two hundred because I'm sending out four hundred invitations." When she heard Marion's tread on the stairs outside her office, Chrystal lowered her voice, cupping the phone with her hand. "Make sure the caviar is fresh, and the vodka freezing. This party has got to be impressive. And, Luther, I want good champagne, too, not that three dollars a bottle stuff you got me for the Christmas party." She laughed softly. "Yeah, they didn't know the difference but these people will, I assure you, and if they aren't drinking the best, they won't think my diamonds are the best."

Her office door opened instantly. The face she raised to Marion's was calm and collected as she hung up the phone. "Yes? Did you need something?"

"No, I don't. But you do."

"And what might that be?"

"A brain," Marion shot back. "Because you don't have one if what I just heard was what I think I heard."

Chrystal raised her chin, her spine three inches from the back of her chair. "Were you eavesdropping?"

"Yes, I was, and I don't believe my ears, either. Were you talking to Luther—Luther, the caterer?"

"Yes."

"And did I hear the words 'champagne' and 'caviar'?"

"Yes."

She shook her head, her hands on her hips. "Are you out of your mind? You're actually having that party, aren't you? After everything that's happened."

"What do you mean?"

"Well, for starters, how about that damn emerald-eating dog?"

"Everything worked out all right. Mrs. Meriweather bought the stone, and I paid Kyoto."

"I know that, but Mr. Maxwell Morris doesn't. If

he knew you'd made that sale, he'd be in here, his hand outstretched.''

"As a matter of fact, we already discussed the issue.''

Marion sat down abruptly. "And?''

"And he's going to help me with the party.'' She waved the list of people Max had given her last night. "These are some friends of his he wants me to include.''

"Well, well. So that's the way the wind is blowing.'' Marion's voice rose, as did her eyebrows.

Chrystal ignored her. "We'll make enough money off this party to pay every debt this store ever had, and then some.''

"You *are* crazy. Neal running off must have tipped you over the edge.''

"Neal doesn't have anything to do with this, Marion.''

"That's for sure. When are you going to wake up and smell the coffee, girl? Spending more money, planning some fancy party, doing every damn thing you can, just to fix his mistakes? You ought to let Max find that worthless brother of yours, and make him pay for all the misery he's caused you.''

Chrystal's anger might have flared last week, but she was beginning to see things differently after her conversation with Max. Still, she answered with more patience than she felt. "I happen to love my brother dearly, and just because he left me in trouble, doesn't mean he's worthless,'' she said mildly.

"Well, even if a miracle happens, and you clear this mess up, what's going to happen the next time? Huh?''

Chrystal's eyes flew to Marion's dark, expressive ones. "Oh, yeah, there's gonna be a next time, and you know it. And the next time, and the next? He's a grown man, Chrystal, and you're not doing him any favors by ruining your own life to try to fix his.''

Chrystal's flushed cheeks felt hot against her fingers as she dropped her face into her hands and rubbed her forehead. ''You may be right, Marion, but I can't do anything about him today.''

The door slammed behind the disgruntled clerk, and Chrystal felt relieved. She didn't want to think about Neal right now. Her mind was too full of Max, there wasn't room for her brother.

Maxwell Morris. The man haunted her. No matter what she did, his dark eyes and chiseled features hovered in the back of her mind. Marion was right about one thing—the deck already belonged to Max because Chrystal had lost her heart.

Why? she moaned. Why now? Love wasn't something she was looking for. She had her business, her dreams, her plans. She didn't need someone whose face would never leave her mind, whose lips she could still taste. The lingering memory delivered more heat to her face as she brought her fingers to her mouth and recalled the overwhelming, almost drowning, sensation of his arms around her on the dance floor last night. Afterwards, his searing kiss had left her numb with desire, and she'd lain awake in her lonely bed until the bright LA sun had broken through the early morning smog.

Max was more than he'd appeared, just as she'd thought that first day when he'd walked into her store and her life. The slick attorney she'd seen was a shell, a façade. The real man underneath the expensive suits and shining long hair was kind and considerate, just as Mrs. Meriweather had tried to convince her. He genuinely cared about his clients and the clinic, and his past bore mute testimony to the fact. Beyond all that, however, was his gut-wrenching sexiness, an absolute animallike appeal she had no defense against.

When he was in the room, others ceased to exist; when he left, so did her interest. She buried her face in her hands once more. Why now?

Chrystal gratefully dropped into the plush chair, the mail she'd picked up still clutched in her hand, the quietness of her bedroom surrounding her like a soft blanket. Sure she'd forgotten something terribly important she'd had to do today, Chrystal sighed and tried to calm her frantic thoughts. For weeks she'd worked later and later, trying to get all the details of the party perfect.

She'd been too busy to even pick up her mail until tonight. With a weary hand, she rubbed her eyes then looked down at the week-old stack of catalogs, bills, and notices. A pale blue air mail envelope grabbed her attention.

At once, Chrystal recognized Neal's sprawling handwriting, then she saw the postmark from Jakarta. He'd mailed the letter over three months ago. She ripped open the envelope, then paused as her heart began to thud. *Is this right?* she asked herself suddenly. *I'm terrified to read this because I know he wants something. The only time I hear from Neal is when he needs me. What's wrong now?*

Her hands began to shake, and Chrystal recalled Marion's words of warning. *There will be a next time, you know it. With Neal, there will always be a next time.* She closed her eyes and tried to calm down, forcing herself to wait until her heart had slowed, and her growing aggravation subsided. She told herself she was jumping to conclusions, letting herself be influenced by Marion's dire warnings. Whatever Neal had to say, she should at least give him the benefit of a doubt before she got too upset. When the pounding had returned to near normal levels, she opened her eyes and slowly unfolded the single thin sheet.

Dear Sis,
Sorry I haven't written until now but I've been really busy working on a great deal. I think things are finally going to pan out, but I've run into a little trouble and was wondering if you could help me. A few thousand dollars is all I need. I know you've got the store going so well by now that you probably won't even miss the money.

Chrystal dropped the letter as if the blue stationery had suddenly caught on fire. She didn't know what made her more mad, Neal asking for money or Neal fulfilling everyone's predictions, the predictions she'd so staunchly disputed.

Her resentment built like steam from a tea kettle. How could he do this to her? Didn't he realize what he was doing? As soon as the thought formed, Chrystal knew the answer. Neal didn't have any idea how his actions affected other people. He was one of those people who was oblivious to anything that happened outside his own small world. And she'd helped perpetuate that attitude, just like Marion and Max had said.

Without thinking, her hand reached out for her checkbook—then stopped. Would sending him money really help? The situation sounded important, she argued with herself, he wouldn't have written if he didn't really need the cash. Besides, he had no idea of the problems she was having at the shop—or did he?

She stood abruptly, sending the lapful of mail tumbling to the floor, her emotions at war with her logic. Something nagged at her, and she knew that something was Max. What would he say when he found out she'd sent her brother money? Even having that question rattle around in her brain bothered her, and she felt torn, her loyalties divided.

Despite his ways, Neal had always been important to her. Her feelings were changing, however, and Chrystal knew she was facing a choice that would affect the rest of her life. He'd always be her brother, but he was her past, her roots. Max was her future.

With an angry groan, she paced the bedroom then caught her reflection in the mirror over her dresser. Dark circles of fatigue shadowed her cheeks, and her hair tumbled about her face in limp strands. Her wrinkled suit hung on her frame like a shirt on a clothesline. She was shocked at how exhausted she looked.

Is this what I want out of life? she found herself asking. *To look old before I am, to worry when I shouldn't, to carry my brother for the rest of my life?*

When her gaze fell away from the glass, her eyes filled with tears and her heart overflowed with sorrow. She would give Neal only one thing: the freedom to fail.

SEVEN

A few weeks later, when she saw the now familiar black limo at the curb, Chrystal rose swiftly. Max had called every day, never showed up without flowers, sent her candy, brought her everything but jewelry. She'd tried to discourage him, but to her secret delight, nothing seemed to work. By the time he'd opened the front door, she stood behind the nearest counter, appearing cool, serene, and in charge—or so she hoped. On the inside, she was growing warm, confused, and totally flustered.

He walked slowly to where she stood, the early morning sun motes dancing about, the silence in the store growing.

"Good morning, Chrystal."

"Hello."

"I came to see how the party plans are going."

"All right."

Their words were spoken out loud, but the real communication was taking place on another plane, another level from which neither one of them seemed able, or willing, to escape. Max's dark eyes stared into Chrystal's gray ones, and the invisible thread between them strengthened, binding them tighter.

The familiar crinkle of the waxy-green, florist paper whispered as he lifted his hand towards her. "This is a 'Star-Gazer' orchid," he said in a throaty voice. "The colors reminded me of you."

Chrystal looked down at the huge flower. The creamy petals were perfection as they disappeared into a deep pink throat. She reached out for it, but when their fingers met, he grasped her hand, refusing to let her go. They stood together, bound by the exotic bloom. He pulled her even closer. "Did you know the ancient Greeks used to make tea from orchid roots?"

"No."

"They used it as an aphrodisiac."

Chrystal swallowed hard. His expression caused a curl of warmth to slowly unfurl in her lower stomach, and the implication of the gift was almost more than she could handle. Nothing could have made her more aware of him than she already was.

"Can we go to your office?"

"Of course."

He followed her up the stairs, and when the door was closed, he spun her around and pressed her against the wall, stretching his body to hers. Without pretense, she clung to him, swept into his embrace by the wave of passion engulfing her.

What is happening? Why am I doing this? Chrystal's thinking side had one second to question her actions before her feeling side took over—or rather, Max's hands and lips took over. In an instant, his mouth covered hers, his tongue insistent.

Deep in her throat, a moan of release and longing

built and escaped in a low murmur. He abandoned the kiss and trailed his lips along her jaw to her ear where, with delicate precision, he outlined the shell with his tongue. Dropping his head to bury his face in her hair, he groaned as though he could feel the same pleasurable pain she did and couldn't stand the agony a moment longer.

He raised his head and kissed her again, this time with even more demand. His hands echoed the pursuit for more, sliding up and down her arms and shoulders with wild abandon. As the kiss deepened, his warm palms traveled up her waist to cup the sides of her full breasts.

Chrystal knew she was out of control, spinning off into a world she didn't want and couldn't have. But she couldn't stop. Her own hands clutched Max's shoulders and pulled him even closer. She wanted more of him, all of him, and the feeling was so unexpected and so overwhelming, she felt faint.

Max finally pulled back, his hands hard on her arms, more questions than answers in his dazed eyes. He looked as disconcerted as she felt, the usually severe face softened, his tie off-center, his suit coat crumpled.

"How can you deny this?" he said, his hoarse voice reflecting her own confusion.

The tension crackled around them like escaping electricity, and Chrystal knew only one small spark was needed to spontaneously ignite the wild conflagration again. "I, I don't think I can much longer. What am I going to do?"

He stepped back, as though he needed to escape, her reply only adding to the thickness around them. Chrystal's legs felt like she'd had the flu for two weeks, and she slid into the recliner on her right.

Max took the chair at her desk, his hand instantly on his tie, pulling the knot straight until he appeared as if nothing had happened. In contrast, Chrystal felt like the world was spinning on a crazy tilt.

"Look—"

"I didn't—"

They both stopped and smiled awkwardly. Finally, he held up his hand. "Ladies first."

"I don't understand all this, Max. I've never, well, what I mean is—"

He pulled his chair closer to hers, then straddled her knees with his and grabbed her hands. For a few seconds, he said nothing but stared at her fingers, almost absent-mindedly stroking the inside of her palms. By the time Max finally looked up, Chrystal felt as though her nerve endings had been set on fire. She struggled to sit still.

"I think 'it' is called love, Chrystal. We've found something that other people only dream about."

She stared at him then sputtered, "But there are so many problems—"

"No," he answered sharply. "Not problems. Hurdles maybe, conflicts, but not problems. Nothing that can't be overcome."

"I don't think you're being realistic."

"Why? Because I'm willing to try and you aren't?"

"I didn't say I wouldn't try, but I have dreams, Max. Goals. Plans. Things I want to accomplish. I don't have the time right now for a relationship. You already said you wanted more than I could give, and I just can't provide you with more."

"Then I'll settle for what I can get. You're too important to me to give up, Chrystal."

His words silenced her, especially because they

echoed her own thoughts. She stood up and moved to the window at the back of the office. Suddenly, a breath of coolness caressed her neck as he lifted up her hair. Before she could object, his lips were trailing over the nape of her neck. He murmured against her skin. "Let me love you, Chrystal. Let me love you."

Tiny tremors of excitement radiated down her spine, and Chrystal felt her will collapsing. "I, I can't think when you do that," she protested feebly.

His breath was hot against the curve of her shoulder. "Good. You think too much, anyway."

"I have to if I want to figure you out."

"Just look for the real person, not the image," he said flatly, surprising her by his words and by moving away from her. "A lot of people think that I *am* my image, but that's all a façade, I promise you." He took the material of his coat between his forefinger and his thumb and shook it. "This is not me. I dress the way I do because it helps me fit in with my clients, that's all. Haven't you learned by now that things aren't always what they seem to be?"

Chrystal looked at him curiously. Even though Max was trying to explain himself, he'd managed to sum up neatly her feelings about Neal. She hated to admit it, even to herself, but her brother wasn't at all what he seemed, and maybe that was why she was having such a hard time accepting the truth.

"What's the matter, sweetheart? You don't look convinced."

Thoughtfully, she looked down at her desk then picked up the telegram from Neal, giving her his flight number and time of arrival.

Max came to her side, his voice low and caring,

but urgent, as if he'd sensed her disquiet. "What is it, Chrystal? Bad news?"

She held out the slip of yellow paper to Max. "This is from Neal. He's coming back to LA. He wrote me months ago and asked for money, but I didn't get the letter till the other day. I got this telegram this morning."

It was Max's turn to look surprised. He took the sheet from her but didn't look at it, staring instead at her. "He asked you for money? After everything he did to you?"

She tried to explain. "I know it's hard for you to understand my loyalty to Neal, but you've never met him, Max. He was born with an abundance of charisma, a real charmer; even if he wasn't my brother, I'd have a hard time saying 'no.' "

Max's exasperated sigh was loud in the tight confines of the office. "So you didn't, did you?"

She felt a flash of irritation, but as soon as it came, the feeling left. Max had more than enough right to assume she'd given in—again. Her voice was low and even. "I never wrote him back. I guess he assumed, and rightly, that I wasn't going to bail him out again." She rose and moved to the window, her back to Max. "You were right. I think it's time for Neal to grow up."

Chrystal dreaded the I-told-you-so she knew was coming, but behind her, she heard Max lay the paper on the desk then step softly to her side. He took one long look at her and folded her into his arms.

She turned and melted into his embrace. His coat, rough under her cheek, smelled like him, a unique combination of aftershave, money, and manliness, and even as distracted as she was over Neal's letter, she felt her heart accelerate. Smoothing her hair,

Max's broad hand cradled the back of her head, and his chest rumbled as he murmured words of consolation. If he'd done anything else, Chrystal wouldn't have cried, but his kindness did her in.

Before she could even fumble for a tissue, like a magician, he pulled a snowy handkerchief from his pocket and handed it to her. In the circle of his arms, she dabbed at her eyes. "Go ahead," she said, "tell me how right you were."

He took a quick step back and grabbed both her shoulders in his hands, giving her a little shake. "Come on, Chrystal. I'm not happy that Neal did what I expected him to. If you'd gotten a letter from him with a giant check in it, I'd have been thrilled for you."

"But he did exactly what you and Marion said he would."

"Yes, that's true, and look at how upset you are. If he'd have proved me wrong, I'd be delighted, because then you wouldn't have tears running down your face now."

She was so upset, his words didn't sink in at first, then slowly she stopped patting her cheeks with the square of cloth, his meaning becoming clear.

"I want what's best for you, Chrystal. I'm not some egomaniac that wants bad things to happen just because I predict they will. Believe me, I'd love to be proved wrong. Unfortunately, when it comes to people like Neal, I've seen enough of them to know exactly what they're going to do—and it's always the same thing. They don't change."

Even though she agreed with Max, Chrystal felt her defenses rise and her back straighten, but before she could speak, she stopped, realizing what she was doing. Her breath came out in a deep sigh. "I guess you're right, but it hurts, Max. It hurts."

His face softened, his dark eyes warm with sympathy. "I know, sweetheart. I wish I could take the pain from you, take it on myself. This isn't fair to you." His jaw tightened suddenly, the lips that had kissed her so tenderly turning into a thin line of anger. "Neal doesn't appreciate you. He doesn't understand what you've done just to protect him. If you hadn't made me promise, I'd like to haul his a—"

"Stop," she said, putting her fingers against his mouth. "This isn't your problem, remember? I told you I'd take care of it, and I will."

He looked down at her, black eyebrows fierce, his chin jutting out stubbornly. "Well, I'd still like to—"

Chrystal shook her head and wrapped her hands around his neck, pulling his face down to hers. For a long moment, she stared into his angry, black eyes, then she kissed him into silence, her lips demanding his full attention. He hesitated a single second then acquiesced.

With an intensity that weakened Chrystal's knees, he pulled her against him, his long torso warming her entire length, his hands seeking more and more as they ranged over her shoulders and back. Finally, his palms travelled lower, and he pulled her even closer, as he hungrily claimed her mouth and then her tongue. She'd started the kiss, but he was definitely going to finish it.

The heat of the moment drove Neal, the store, everything from Chrystal's mind, and she felt her body responding in a way it never had before. Nerve endings she didn't even know she had were screaming, and she found herself pressing against Max with an astonishing abandonment. Like the hot Santa Ana winds that swept the California hills, her passion ignited and burned everything in its course; reason, logic, common sense, all burst into flames and disappeared.

When Max finally pulled his lips from hers, Chrystal's eyes were too heavy to open, and she swayed blindly in his embrace. At length, he spoke, his voice the husky whisper she'd come to love. "Come to my house for dinner tonight, Chrystal. I want to make it special, right, just for us. I'll send the car."

He wasn't talking about their meal, and she knew it. She nodded mutely, unable to do anything but acquiesce.

As Max's limousine climbed the steep drive to his house, Chrystal ran her long strand of pearls between her fingers, touching each individual bead in nervousness. The movement formed a gleaming, iridescent stream of beauty, and the smooth coolness soothed her momentarily.

She'd worried about everything since they'd made the date for this evening; what to wear (under her casual sweater and suede skirt, the sexiest underwear Rodeo Drive had to offer covered her with utter disregard for utility), what to bring (after great deliberation, she'd finally selected a bottle of Puligny Montrachet, 1980), even what they'd talk about (she had a feeling there probably wouldn't be a lot of talking).

Chrystal knew it was the last worry that had her palms wet and her mouth dry. The tension between them had grown daily, and despite her very best intentions, she knew she'd fallen in love with Maxwell Morris. Both of them were ready to acknowledge that, she realized with a start. It was time to quit shadow-boxing.

The car glided to a smooth stop, and up front, Williams stepped out. Sliding across the smooth leather, Chrystal gathered her coat, her bottle of wine, and her nervousness as he opened her door. The California evening had turned cooler, and she involuntarily shivered as she followed him up the path.

Before they reached the front door, it opened. Max was outlined from behind with soft lights and he held out his arms as Chrystal stepped inside. Williams discreetly disappeared.

"Welcome to my home, darling." His embrace was warm, soft, loving. Chrystal felt as though she'd walked into another fairy tale.

The kiss he gave her was more than real, however. It left her even shakier than she had been before. They separated, and when he looked down at her face, his eyes were black with desire. "I'm glad you came, Chrystal. I've dreamed about seeing you here, but I wanted to wait until the time was perfect—just right. I wanted you to *want* to come."

She nodded quietly and stepped back out of his arms. He moved to one side, and when he did she got her first glimpse of the room beyond the entry.

For the first time in her life, Chrystal understood what it meant to be completely breathless. Shock then delight washed over her in waves of disbelief as she moved soundlessly into the vast room.

The entire back wall, at least thirty feet, was glass. Beyond the almost invisible barrier, the world seemed to stretch before her eyes. "Oh, Max," she said in a whisper, "it's incredible."

She dropped her coat on a white leather couch in

the center of the room, set the bottle of wine on a nearby table, and walked, as if called silently, to the vast window. Whichever direction she looked, lights twinkled and blinked as if teasing her. Los Angeles, the city so well-known for its ability to create reality where none existed, lie at her feet in all its natural beauty.

Without a sound, he came up behind her and put his arms around her, his chest warm and reassuring against her back. He rested his cheek against her hair, the light scent of his aftershave wrapping her in a sensual wave of anticipation.

"Sometimes I sit here for hours," he said quietly. "When it's been a good day, and the air is clean, I can look out and see forever." His embrace tightened and she felt him bury his face in the curve of her shoulder. They stood together, without speaking, while minutes passed. Chrystal knew she would never forget this night.

Finally, his arms dropped with a reluctant whisper, and he took her hand instead. "Let me show you the rest of the house."

"Is it all this spectacular?"

"Well, I have to admit, this is the best view, but I wouldn't turn down the others, either."

They moved through the living room and for the first time, Chrystal saw the giant fireplace on the wall opposite the window. Behind a curved glass screen, a smoldering fire glimmered with sensual promise, throwing its flickering lights across the palest of rugs.

He led her past a giant dining room, dark with high ceilings. Silver trays and crystal stemware sparkled from behind leaded glass doors on a massive breakfront, but Max kept going, ignoring the table of inlaid wood and richly upholstered chairs. They entered the kitchen.

The pristine, contemporary look she'd expected wasn't there, but Chrystal was not disappointed. This was a lived-in room, gigantic, with another fireplace at one end where a small table had been set for two. She started to speak, to tell him how much she loved it, but suddenly her eyes were drawn to a nearby window.

Stepping closer, Chrystal saw the glimmer of the kitchen lights reflected on a large, glass enclosure. Finally, something that didn't surprise her—a greenhouse!

Delighted, she turned and smiled. "Now I know all about you, Maxwell Morris—you haven't been buying those flowers—you grew all those right here, didn't you?"

"Most of them," he admitted, moving to stir something delicious smelling in a simmering pot on the stove. "I don't mention my hobby a lot—" he glanced up with a grin. "It's incongruent with my sharklike image."

She turned back to the glass but instead of looking outside, she watched the watery reflection of the man behind her as he lifted his spoon to taste. She shocked herself by envying the silver in his hand as he let his tongue glide over the smooth metal.

She forced her thoughts back to the mirrored impression. The *real* Max had indeed surprised her, just as he'd promised. She'd been so overwhelmed with the image, the aura of power, that she'd missed the gentler side, the romantic side. The flowers should have given him away, but she'd assumed they too had been part of his slick presentation.

She turned. "You could have told *me*."

"Old habits die hard, I guess. I spent so many years trying to escape flowers that I stay quiet out of habit."

"What do you mean?"

He put the spoon down on the side of the stove. "My mother and father ran a florist shop. When I was growing up, I had to make all the deliveries, and I hated it then." He shook his head, remembering. "I never saw the flowers themselves. I was too busy trying to keep the vases upright, not crush the blooms, get the right arrangement to the right location."

He walked around the cooking island and filled two wine glasses from a bottle he'd already opened, handing one to Chrystal then sipping from his own. "I didn't really appreciate them till later—after my folks died."

The regret in his voice touched her. "Didn't appreciate the flowers or your parents?"

He raised one eyebrow. "Both." Another sip then he looked back at her. "You've liked the flowers then?"

"Oh, yes, Max. They've all been gorgeous but now to know that you grew some of them—that makes them even more special."

Smiling, he walked up to her and put his arm around her waist. Taking her glass and setting it down on the cabinet, he turned her back toward the hall. As they passed the smaller table, he said, "I hope you don't mind eating in here," he said.

"I wouldn't have it any other way," she said slowly. "As long as you're sitting on the other side of the table."

He grinned. "You might not say that after you taste my cooking."

"I'm not worried."

"Good. Then let me show you the rest of the house."

They turned and left the kitchen area, passing once more through the den. Chrystal's eyes were pulled to the wall of glass. The view hadn't disappeared; in fact, as the sky had turned darker, the panorama looked even better.

"I don't think I'd ever leave this room," she said as they kept going. "I'd eat, I'd sleep—"

They walked into a massive bedroom, and Chrystal swallowed the rest of her words. It was hard to believe, but the vista was more stunning in here. Before them, a huge bed, flanked by twin tables, faced the windows, its padded headboard resting against a low half-wall that curved outward in the center of the room, matching the curve of the glass. The whole ensemble was elevated, with built-in lights glowing softly on the two steps leading upwards. Behind the bed and facing them as they entered, a small but comfortable grouping of chairs surrounded another fireplace.

Chrystal ignored the chairs and walked up the two steps slowly, going directly to the foot of the bed. She sank down and sat on the wide bench, padded to match the headboard, that rested at the base of the bed. Max joined her.

"I can't imagine living with such a glorious view." She turned to him, his face barely visible in the low light. "Just think, it's the first thing you see when you wake up and the last thing you see before you close your eyes. It's perfect."

He took her chin in his hand and slowly shook his head. "No." His grip tightened gently. "It'd be perfect if you were lying beside me."

Chrystal closed her eyes to see better the delightful image his words brought to mind, and when she did, Max's lips danced across her own. The butterfly touch, the warmth, the brief impression of wine he'd already had made her realize the view had blocked out all the other wonderful sensations that were now beginning to assault her.

He ran his fingers over her hair to the bareness of her neck and began to murmur, his lips abandoning her mouth to trail down the line of her jaw.

"God, you smell good. There's no flower on this earth that could compete with you."

Chrystal was too immersed in the impressions now flooding her senses to reply. From the back of the house, the low, sweet sounds of a saxophone played softly, and behind them the fire popped and whistled in accompaniment. The slightly smokey smell made her feel warm and comfortable, but Max's mouth and hands were pulling her away from any kind of relaxation.

He tucked one strand of her hair behind her ear then gently kissed the outer edge of it. She could hear his breath. It was slow and steady now but she had a feeling it wouldn't be for long.

"Chrystal," he murmured then repeated her name again, this time pulling back enough to look in her eyes. "Chrystal—your name contradicts you."

"What do you mean?" His fingers massaged the nape of her neck and his other hand dropped lower to curve around her waist. Her breath quickened as his palm slipped under her sweater.

"Crystal is cold, transparent, fragile." He bent his head again to hers and left a track of kisses up the line of her jaw to just below her ear. When he lifted his lips to stare into her eyes, Chrystal's heart lunged into a definitely irregular beat. "You aren't like that at all," he whispered.

His hand rose slowly, and as his fingers swept over her right, silk-covered breast and lingered, Chrystal's breath came in sharply with pleasure.

"I can feel your warmth—your heart," he said. "You definitely are not cold."

For two more heartbeats, his fingers stayed motionless, then he lifted his hand and traced a circle around the swell beneath the silk. The delicate touch made Chrystal want to squirm but his mesmerizing stare kept her perfectly still.

"You're not transparent, either." One finger slowly followed the under curve of her breast to her left side then up to her shoulder. With lazy precision, he drew a line of desire from her shoulder back down. Chrystal's mouth opened slightly, and she licked her suddenly dry lips. "You're a very complex lady with complicated feelings and desires—and I'm falling in love with each and every one of them."

In the darkness of the luxurious bedroom, a tingling awareness took possession of her, fostered by more than just his words. Beneath her outstretched fingers, the steel of Max's leg flexed as he moved closer. Chrystal wondered if she were dreaming.

"And you're definitely not fragile." He pushed her gently back until she was stretched out on the deeply quilted bedspread. "You're a tough, gutsy woman and I love you, Chrystal."

The compliment meant more to Chrystal than any of the flowery words Max could have used. He'd told her the two magic things she'd always wanted that one perfect man to say—"I respect you" and "I love you."

She wrapped her hands in his hair and pulled him

down closer to her. The moon had come up since they'd entered the room, and the sterling light fell across the bed in a long shadow. Max was darkness; she was light.

"I love you, too, Max," she breathed. "And I want to show you."

His lips took hers and claimed them for his own as the length of his body pressed against hers, hard against soft, straight against curved. Unconsciously, she pushed closer to him, her soft breasts rubbing against his chest with an almost painful urgency.

When he finally lifted his head, she actually felt dizzy.

"I want to undress you."

She nodded her agreement and he slid to the end of the bed, pulling her with him. His face was still shadowed but Chrystal could feel the desire in him. Like a misty cloud, it enveloped her also. She breathed deeply, an effort to calm her racing heart, but instead she breathed in Max's scent, and her pulse reacted with a quickened beat.

He kissed her lightly while his hands reached under her long sweater and around to the back of her skirt. The rasp of the zipper, a draft of air, and the buttery leather fell to her feet. She kicked it aside, along with her shoes.

He smiled in the darkness, never breaking their eye contact. His hands were warm on her waist, his fingers strong and wide. "Turn about is fair play," he said.

Her fingers went to the bottom of his soft cotton sweater and as she pulled it upwards, he lifted his arms and helped her. The V of his chest was broader and wider than she'd expected, his arms muscular and tight.

Breathing in, Chrystal laid her hands against the steel of his chest. He was warm and beneath her fingers she could feel his heart beating. The rhythm matched her own, fast and heavy with need. He laced her hands with his, pressing her fingertips into the dark mat of hair dusting his chest between his nipples. She dropped her lips to his chest and outlined each dark spot with her tongue. Instantly, he drew his breath and closed his eyes, squeezing her hands with his.

A low groan built deep in his chest, and Chrystal laid her face against his warmth, feeling the sound before she heard it. "Oh, God," he breathed, "what are you doing to me?"

She tilted her head and smiled. "I haven't even started yet."

"I don't know if I can stand this," he said. "I'm not a young man any more, you know."

She arched her eyebrows. "Well, for an old guy, you look like you're in pretty good shape to me."

Grinning, he took the bottom of her sweater in his hands. "Well, let's see what kind of shape you're in, sweetheart."

The ivory pullover slipped over her head, and suddenly Chrystal's shyness returned. She stood before him, the creamy silk camisole and panties leaving little to the imagination. His eyes widened with delight then darkened with something else—and she forgot her reserve.

He caressed her, his fingers moving sensually across her back, then he slowly slipped the straps of the camisole down. It joined her skirt and sweater on the floor.

"My God," he whispered, "you're like one of those beautiful South Sea pearls you sell. All ivory perfection, smooth, silky.'' He licked his lips and pulled the bottom one in between his teeth then spoke. ''If I hold you in my hand, will you turn warm, too?''

''Try it and find out,'' she breathed.

His hands grasped the curve of her arms then slid to her waist. Finally they went lower to the sweet flare of her hips as his teeth nipped lightly across her shoulder. Warmth and cold, wet and dry, soft and rough, the contrasts bombarded Chrystal's body and mind.

His lips began a trail of hot desire down her now bare breasts, and Chrystal couldn't restrain a moan of excitement as he took first one and then the other nipple into his mouth. His mouth was warm and wet and so was she.

He slid down until he was on his knees. Chrystal buried her hands in his hair as he kissed her breasts, her stomach, her thighs. Mindless murmurs of passion built in her throat then died in a gasp as his mouth searched out her most sensitive spots.

Finally, at the point where she could take no more, he rose and slipped off the rest of his clothes. She knew she was reaching the limit of her own restraint and he was, too. As if he'd read her mind, he wrapped his arms around her and gracefully lifted her up, placing her on the bed beside him. The rising beat of his passion changed, and the urgency that grew between them could no longer be held back.

He laid down beside her, then pulled her on top of him. She straddled his waist, her hair forming a curtain of silky strands on either side of their faces, her breasts suspended over his chest, the sensitive tips brushing his own nipples with painful anticipation.

Unrestrained, Chrystal tightened her knees against the hardened outer muscles of his thighs. Instantly she felt the rough hair on his legs scratch against her own smooth skin. Every inch of her body was experiencing new sensations, and slowly but irrevocably she felt her tenuous control slipping. Gently, slowly, Max increased the pressure of his hands on her hips, forcing her downwards until he slid inside her.

She closed her eyes as pounding waves of desire took hold and drew her under. The silken touch of the sheets, the maddening scent of their shared arousal, even Max's hoarse voice urging her on, all disappeared in the undertow of her passion.

Finally, in one last, desperate second, Chrystal opened her eyes and stared into Max's black gaze. His face mirrored her own pleasure. She smiled then closed her eyes once more, allowing the wash of pleasure to carry her into total insensibility. For endless moments, the heat between them throbbed then finally they both shuddered, inert, voiceless, and disbelieving in the intensity of their love.

Slowly, their breathing returned to normal, and Chrystal loosened her hands from Max's shoulders and raised up slightly. Deep indentions marked his skin where she clutched him, but somehow she didn't think he'd mind. Lines of moonlight crisscrossed his face and Chrystal lifted her thumb to trace their path across his cheeks.

He opened his eyes and the tension eased slowly from his body, his legs relaxing beneath her. The fingers that had gripped her hips rose and lightly cupped her face. Staring at her, he rubbed his thumb over her bottom lip as though he wanted to imprint the sensation onto his mind, never to be forgotten.

"Lie down beside me," he finally said, "I want that perfection we talked about—the view *and* you."

When she walked into the office the next day, Chrystal knew she must look different. No one could feel as different as she did and not *look* different, also. The ghost of the previous day's passion hovered in the air above her desk. She stood in the same spot she'd stood yesterday when Max had kissed her so thoroughly, and without any warning at all, a wave of desire swamped her. She sat down abruptly, her knees going out from under her.

They never got around to dinner that night. In fact, she'd didn't even go home until late the following day. She felt deliciously wicked—Max had that kind of effect on her.

How could one man be so disruptive? Her life had been organized, well-thought out, together. Max had taken it, turned it upside down, and shaken it up. She'd been so wiped out—even before the date—that she'd left the store and hadn't even cleaned off her desk—something Chrystal never did. No telling what she'd forget to do now.

She groaned and rubbed her forehead as if she could erase the memories of yesterday's intimacies. The things they'd done, the feelings they'd shared— they were almost too sweet, too painful. Finally, the sight of Neal's telegram brought her back to earth. She opened her center desk drawer and shoved the hateful piece of yellow paper inside.

His plane was due in the night of the party. He would just have to find his own way home; she couldn't leave her guests just to pick him up. Besides, she wasn't even sure she wanted to see him.

What she'd told Max yesterday was the truth; Neal *had* to grow up. It was time.

Chrystal grimly pursed her lips and turned to the bills on her desk, determined to put Neal and Max out of her mind. But for the rest of the day that proved impossible. Nothing could penetrate the daze of desire and need Max had wrapped her in.

Late that afternoon, the door to the shop opened, and when Chrystal saw who came in, she grinned broadly. Here was one of the few people who'd be able to take her mind back to business. Cece Burnett, the New York dealer Chrystal had called the minute she'd decided to do the party, stood uncertainly in the front of the store, her hundred pound frame grossly outweighed by the enormous black display cases resting on rollers beside her.

A black dress—Cece only wore black—hung loosely from her narrow shoulders to the tips of her ankle boots, barely touching her childlike body, and a huge black hat, complete with veil, perched on top of her head giving the slight woman the appearance of a tiny, startled bird. She blinked rapidly, her glance darting over the shop until she finally saw Chrystal.

"Ohmigod—this *is* the right place—Lord, I thought I'd never find this dump—here take these cases, I've got to go pay that godforsaken taxi driver—I swear he brought me to Rodeo Drive via Anaheim—God, I hate California, the sun's so bright." She turned around and flew out the door, digging through the huge purse she wore strapped across her chest like a *pistolero's* ammunition belt.

As the bell tinkled behind the frazzled dealer, Chrystal laughed and started forward, rescuing the abandoned cases and pushing them before her to the back of the store. She'd known Cece for years, but the tiny woman's rapid fire conversations always managed to surprise her. Chrystal secretly suspected the dealer talked that way because it never gave the buyer a chance to say "No."

Marion came out from behind the counter and helped Chrystal pull the first of the cases into the downstairs vault. "Who, or should I say, what was that?"

"Cece Burnett," Chrystal answered. "She's the pearl and gold dealer I told you about." She grabbed the second case and pushed the heavy unit in behind the first one, patting the black top as she went. "These babies are full now, but after tomorrow night, they'll all be empty." She raised her eyes to Marion's. "And our cash drawer will be overflowing."

Marion's sigh filled the safe. "I don't know. She doesn't look like she's got a brain in her head, much less one for business. You sure about her?" The black woman's stare went back to the front of the store where the door had reopened.

Cece's nonstop conversation with herself was audible even in the vault. "We're back here," Chrystal called before turning to Marion. "Just wait. You won't believe the pieces she has in here."

Two hours later, Marion was as much in awe of Cece as Chrystal hoped all her customers would be the following night. "This is truly incredible," Marion admitted. "I've got to have those gold loops for myself, the ones with the tourmalines on the side. They're wonderful."

"Well, thank you, my dear, they are different, aren't they, and they'll look so wonderful with your hair, I do think, though, you know, they might be better with topaz for you—kinda matches your eyes better than the tourmaline, I'll tell you what, let me do two pair, one of each, then you can decide which you like better, of course, you'd be foolish not to buy both . . .''

Chrystal smiled and stepped outside the safe. She knew by the time Cece was finished, Marion would have six new pairs of earrings. That was exactly why Chrystal had picked Cece to come: Not only did she have incredible talent with jewelry, she was a whiz at selling.

And selling was exactly what Chrystal had to make sure occurred. If there had been any doubts in her mind about her situation, the bills she'd paid this morning dispelled them like the sun had the early morning smog.

Max's payment schedule was more than generous, but still, Plotsky's debt hung over her head like a sharpened sword, and Chrystal knew she'd never feel comfortable until he'd been paid. The party *had* to be a success—it was the only hope she had of retiring the obligation quickly.

And after she dealt with Mr. Plotsky, there would be Max. What kind of man would be willing to wait for a woman who was so dedicated to a business that she put her store before her personal life? Not to mention a woman with the family baggage she carried. Max had never struck her as patient, but then, there seemed to be a lot about Max she hadn't realized at first—and despite her best efforts, the more she learned about him, the more she learned about herself, and the deeper she fell in love.

EIGHT

The store looked perfect. Graceful arrangements of white roses with pink tips decorated strategic points on the counter tops, while in one corner, the harpist Chrystal had hired for the evening softly tuned her instrument. A long, low table beneath the windows held a small ice sculpture and silver trays piled high with glistening caviar. Tuxedoed waiters received last minute instructions from the caterer as Chrystal nervously surveyed the room once more.

Yes, the store looked perfect. Her reflection, however, captured in the mirrored walls behind the counter, showed lavender shadows beneath her eyes and a nervous hand parting her bangs. Chrystal quickly dropped her fingers and shifted her shoulder blades backwards, with a mental shake of her head. The store looked perfect, the party would go great, she looked fine—the positive mantra rang in her head but did no good. She couldn't shake the feeling of anxiety that had dogged her all afternoon.

All the arrangements had been made, everything

was in place. There was absolutely no reason for her to feel so anxious, but she did, and she had no idea why. Like a toothache, the feeling that something was not right nagged at her.

She frowned and tried to shake the worry, turning her attention instead to watching Cece and Marion huddling behind the counter. They were arguing over how to lay out Cece's precious goods when the door opened, and Max walked in. As if the room had suddenly telescoped, Chrystal's vision narrowed to the tall, well-built man.

He approached her slowly, reminding her once more of an elegant black cat on the prowl. His hair was slicked back, the ponytail discreet, and in the black satin lapel of his tuxedo, a single blood-red rose lay in startling contrast. He looked every inch the successful attorney—and sensual lover—that he was.

He neared, and her heart began a staccato pounding. She automatically closed the distance between them and moved into his open arms as if they had been married for twenty years. No one else existed in the room when Max bent his head to hers and kissed her firmly on the mouth, his hands warm against her back. Chrystal clung to him, reluctant to part even as he pulled back. In his arms, she felt right with the world.

"You look unbelievable," he whispered. "What do you say we blow off this party and go back to my house instead?"

"Don't tempt me, please," she said. "I might never return, and I'm nervous enough to do just that."

"Nervous? You?" He draped one arm around her shoulder and surveyed the room. "How can you be nervous? Everything looks wonderful, you have absolutely nothing to be afraid of. I'm sure the party will be a great success.''

"You have more faith than I do." She shook her head and frowned. "I'm having some real doubts, Max. I don't know, but I just feel . . .''

"Scared?"

"Yes, but something else. I'm not sure what." She took a deep breath. "I know it sounds silly, but I have this feeling that something's not right. Like I've forgotten something important, a detail I overlooked. I don't know." She looked up at him, searching for reassurance.

He smiled and pulled her closer. "Party jitters, that's all.''

"I hope you're right," she murmured. The front door opened again, this time to admit the first of her guests.

The room quickly filled, and Chrystal greeted each new arrival. Women in sparkling gowns and twinkling jewels darted around the shop like glittering butterflies, the men beside them providing encouragement and money. Max's friends were lavish in both.

When Mrs. Meriweather arrived, Chrystal kissed the air near the older woman's powdered cheek and whispered her thanks. "I'm so grateful you came and for all your help. The list of names you gave me was fantastic. Almost all of them came.''

The matron smiled regally and patted her helmet of gray hair. "My dear, that's the very least I could do. Why, you've been so gracious to me, especially after Little Bit's, uh, problem. What else could I do?''

"Did you bring him tonight?"

"Of course, of course." She turned around, her generous breasts moving before her like twin cannons. "Charles, over here," she demanded.

The long-suffering chauffeur stepped quickly to her side, and Chrystal got her first glimpse of the small, silk pillow he carried. Sitting on top of the fringed and tasseled cushion like a miniature four-legged pasha, Little Bit gazed serenely at the well-heeled crowd. A thick gold chain surrounded the dog's tiny neck, and when he lifted his chin, Chrystal gasped.

"Mrs. Meriweather, is that what I think it is?"

The stately matron beamed with glee, obviously delighted at Chrystal's horror. "Yes, doesn't he look positively gorgeous?"

Chrystal swallowed hard. She didn't know whether to laugh hysterically or weep with disbelief. "That, that's the emerald you bought for Gloria."

Mrs. Meriweather's snort of disgust revealed her thoughts succinctly. "I gave the situation a great deal of thought, Chrystal, and I realized that Little Bit has many more redeeming qualities than my daughter-in-law, so I decided to let him have the stone. I think the pendant looks far superior around his neck than it would around hers anyway, and besides, he obviously had a certain, shall we say, affinity for the stone."

Chrystal shook her head, one finger under her eye to catch the tears of laughter. "You are something else, Mrs. Meriweather."

Chrystal reached over and scratched the tiny dog's ears, and he tilted his head to maximize his pleasure, the fantastic emerald shimmering in the low lights of the store. "You're definitely the top dog here tonight, Little Bit," she said with a chuckle.

Suddenly Mrs. Meriweather's soft cheeks turned pink with delight, Chrystal assumed from her pleasure with the little dog, then Max's tall form appeared at her side. In amusement, Chrystal watched him bend over and place a resounding kiss on the plump matron's lips.

"Elizabeth," he said with obvious pleasure, "you look so lovely tonight." He leaned over closer. "What are you doing after the party? Any chance I might get lucky?"

She turned a deeper shade of rose and playfully fluffed her lace-edged handkerchief at him, a haze of Joy drifting to Chrystal's nose. "You naughty boy," she gushed, "if I were twenty years younger, I might be tempted, but of course, we know you're somewhat taken now, aren't you?" Her black raisinlike eyes darted between him and Chrystal.

Now it was Chrystal's turn to blush as Max moved closer to her side and hugged her to him. "Yes," he said without hesitation in his voice, "I am taken, very much so."

"I knew it," she beamed, "I told Charles just the other day, didn't I, Charles? that you two were an item." The chauffeur nodded automatically then steadied the disgruntled dog on top of the shaking cushion as she continued. "You look perfect together, if I do say so. Just like the late Arthur One and I did together." She blinked rapidly then smiled at Chrystal.

Max broke the moment smoothly. "I got your check yesterday. I really appreciate your donation to the clinic, Elizabeth. The money is going to go a long way with our new child care facility."

"Wonderful, wonderful, Maxwell. When I heard about the idea, I couldn't believe someone had never thought of it before. You are a genius, you know that, don't you?''

He grinned and shook his head. "Thank you, but that may be stretching the truth, Elizabeth.''

She beamed broadly then leaned closer in an air of confidence. "I heard that Hiram Plotsky made a major contribution, too. Is that true?''

Max quickly cut his eyes toward Chrystal then faced the older woman again. "At the risk of ruining his less than sterling reputation, I have to tell you the truth, Elizabeth. Yes, Hiram gave very generously to the child care center in return for a little favor I did for him.''

Chrystal felt her eyes widen. Max had told her he'd handled Hiram's paperwork as a "favor"; now she understood. She wanted to know more, but just as she started to question him, she felt Marion's light touch. The black woman leaned over and whispered in her ear. "Dr. Smythe's wife wants you. She's trying to talk him into a major buy over here, and I think you could close the deal.''

Chrystal nodded then turned back to Mrs. Meriweather and Max. "Please excuse me." She looked pointedly at Max. "Duty calls, but I want to hear more about this later.''

She edged her way through the crowded room, the conversation still fresh in her mind. Max and Mrs. Meriweather obviously had a mutual admiration society going, but their cooperation went deeper, too, as did Max and Hiram's. How often, she wondered, did Max trade work for charity donations.

How could she have ever thought him heartless and cold? She nodded and smiled at her customers, but her mind was still on Max. The more she got to know him, the less he fit the mold she'd first stuck him in. First the clinic, now a childcare facility? Suddenly, she made the connection when she remembered the look of guilt he'd worn while telling her about the case in San Diego. The murderer he'd represented and gotten acquitted had killed a mother and child. Was this facility Max's way of atoning for their death?

Chrystal put aside her thoughts of Max and smiled as she reached Mrs. Smythe's side. Quickly, she began to point out the finer points of the ring the woman and her husband were examining. No matter how hard she tried, though, a part of Chrystal was still on the other side of the room, with Max.

Dr. Smythe had his checkbook out in record time, and Chrystal waded back into the crowd, trying to see everyone and say hello. Her mind wasn't really on the task, though, and she found herself searching the throng for a tall figure with a ponytail.

How could one man dominate her mind so much? She'd been planning this party for weeks, and now, right in the midst of it, all she could do was think about Max.

Chrystal took a glass of champagne from a passing waiter and let her lips curve upward as she thought about the invitation Max had extended earlier. An automatic shiver of excitement skipped up her back. Her progress slowed to a halt, the party forgotten, as Chrystal permitted herself the luxury of remembering her night with Max.

Like water parting around an island, the mob eddied past her, a motionless figure in the center of the room. Max was the most attractive man she'd ever known, and now that her thoughts of desire had been released, Chrystal couldn't hold back. As she recalled their passion, her desire to repeat the night almost overwhelmed her. All of her efforts were needed to remain where she was and not push through everyone in search of him.

With great discipline, Chrystal forced her feet to stay still and her mind to calm down. She was successful with the former but failed with the latter. Like a spider trapped in a web of desire, the more she struggled, the more hopeless the situation turned. Relentless images of tangled limbs and crushed sheets bombarded her, and she felt helpless to stop the sensual mental movie playing out behind her closed eyes.

She swayed in the crush, her body warm and flushed. Dozens of expensive perfumes scented the dense air around her, and she struggled to breathe. Her breasts, straining against the jeweled bodice of her gown, felt full and tight, and her fingers pulled at the Mandarin collar lying close against her throat. Even the cold glass of champagne she clutched in one trembling hand didn't cool her.

As if she'd telegraphed her sensations to him, Max magically appeared by her side. The reality of the crowd faded into the background of her consciousness, the noise of a hundred voices disappearing, as Chrystal stared into his hot, dark eyes.

Her own desire was mirrored in those black depths, but it was the silent threat of domination also there that made her shiver. To let him take control, to allow his natural mastery, to permit the ancient male versus female battle to take place was the only thought that filled her mind. For once, Chrystal wanted to abandon everything, all of her responsibilities, her obligations, herself, and she revealed that to Max with one exposing look.

He didn't touch her; he didn't have to. Instead,

the invisible thread that had always connected them strengthened and wrapped them irrevocably together.

Slowly, inevitably, he closed his hand about her own and guided her champagne flute to her coral lips, tipping the glass until she was forced to drink the pale gold liquid. Her throat opened, and the cold bubbles slid down with a shock.

When she'd swallowed, he pulled the glass away from her mouth then turned the rim until the pale outline of her lipstick faced him. His eyes never left hers as he brought the crystal to his own mouth, and with his tongue, deliberately licked the waiting drops of champagne from the edge. For a single heartbeat, he paused then abruptly tipped the flute and downed the remaining liquid.

He leaned down and whispered one word. Chrystal nodded her agreement.

"Later?" had said it all.

During the evening, every time Chrystal looked up, Max was watching her, waiting for her. His intensity made her shiver, and the anticipation building in the pit of her stomach did little to lessen the anxiety already there over the party. As the event progressed, however, Chrystal knew her debts were history. Dr. Smythe's wife purchased the most expensive piece Cece had brought, Mrs. Meriweather found a new bauble for her daughter-in-law, to replace the emerald she never received, and Max's friends bought everything else.

For the first time since she'd purchased Cummins, Chrystal felt like she could draw a breath of relief. As she drifted through the crowd, she knew by the way people were talking that the store and her inventory were impressing them all. With a tiny smile that hinted at her elation, she walked up to Max.

"The party's going quite well, don't you think?" she whispered.

"That's a slight understatement," he said. "I can't tell what's going faster, the diamonds or the caviar."

"And you thought this was, let me see, I believe the word you used was 'irresponsible'?"

His mouth curved into an easy grin. "So I was wrong. Sue me."

"I just might do that," she threatened. "I do know a good attorney."

"Yes, but is he a shark? That's what you really need in these kinds of cases, you know."

She tucked her arm inside his and snuggled closer, the expensive fabric of his tuxedo smooth beneath her fingers, the steely muscles of his arm hard under the cloth. She swallowed hard and tried to concentrate on the conversation. "A shark?" she repeated. "More like a lamb in shark's clothing."

"I think that's 'wolf.' A 'wolf' in lamb's clothing."

She grinned. "That, too."

He smiled but ran his hand over his slicked-back hair, looking about the room impatiently. When he spoke again, his voice was lower, huskier. "How much longer is this affair going to last?"

She glanced down at her diamond-encrusted watch. "At least three more hours—"

"Three hours? Are you kidding?" he interrupted, his eyes unbelieving. "You couldn't possibly get another warm body in here, and these people can't stay forever."

"I invited two shifts."

"Excuse me?"

Chrystal leaned over and kissed his slightly rough cheek. "Come on, sweetheart. You know as well as I do that there are two crowds in LA—the before-dinner shoppers and the late-night crowd. I didn't want to miss anyone so I scheduled one group before nine and another for later." She nodded toward a couple dressed in matching leather outfits. "See, a few more flamboyant types—early, late-nighters—have already arrived."

"Three hours," he repeated morosely as Marion interrupted again, and Chrystal felt herself propelled toward another anxious buyer. Her body responded, but her mind stayed with Max.

In another hour, Chrystal's cheeks ached from smiling, and her feet were screaming for release from the four-inch heels she'd encased them in. She slipped up to Marion's side. "I've got to have a break. Can you handle this for just a little while?"

The saleswoman's face broke into a generous smile. "Are you kidding, honey? I can take in money like this all day long and never get tired." She waved her hand upwards. "You go on upstairs. Rest a bit. If I need you, I know where to find you."

"Thanks a bunch. I won't take too long." She glanced around quickly. "Have you seen Max?"

"Last time I saw him, the man was selling a string of pearls to some high society lady. Can you beat that?" Marion swiveled her head left and right. "Come to think of it, I haven't seen him in the last ten, fifteen minutes. It's so crowded in here, though, I couldn't find the Lord if I had to."

Chrystal grinned and turned. "If you see him—Max, not the Lord—tell him where I am. Okay?"

Marion returned the grin. "Sure thing, baby."

Another fifteen minutes passed as she worked her

way through the crowd, but Chrystal finally reached the stairs in the back of the shop. At the top, without turning on the light, she slipped inside her office and softly closed the door.

The quietness engulfed her like an expensive fur coat, and it felt just as wonderful. Where her dress was cut out to reveal a pale oval of smooth shoulders and back, the cooler air of the empty room caressed her feverish skin in welcome relief. Instantly she felt better as she raised first one foot and then the other, pulling off her white pumps with a loud sigh of relief. Clutching the shoes in her right hand, she padded to the window that looked down over the party, the bright lights below providing a dim glow in the office, her body relaxing but her nerves still on edge.

"What took you so long?"

Chrystal gasped, dropped her shoes, and spun around, her hand at her throat, her eyes searching the darkness. "What the hell—"

"Hey, slow down, baby. It's only me."

Max's deep voice registered for the first time, and Chrystal leaned weakly against the desk, relieved yet still tense.

He stood up then, and came closer to her, but made no effort to touch her. Without her shoes on, Chrystal realized the discrepancy in their heights. She looked up into his eyes. "You scared me half to death. What are you doing up here, anyway?"

His voice was a deep rumble. "Waiting for you."

Her heart had slowed as soon as she had recognized Max, but his closeness forced it back into a faster beat. Her reply sounded breathless, even to her own ears. "How'd you know I'd come?"

"I didn't, but I'm a gambling man so I thought

I'd take a chance." His hand rose slowly and with the back of one finger, he gently followed the curve of her jaw, from her chin to just behind her ear. "How about you, Chrystal. Do you ever gamble?"

She swallowed hard but didn't break her steady gaze. Soft light from the window outlined Max's face, leaving his eyes in a deep shadow, but Chrystal didn't need illumination to see his desire. She could hear the need in his voice and feel the want in his touch. "Yes," she answered slowly, "if the odds are good."

His fingers snuck under the curtain of her hair to cup the nape of her neck, and when he answered, his breath was warm and sweet against her cheek. "Baby, this is the surest bet you'll ever make."

Pulling her towards him, Max lowered his head and melded his lips with hers. The velvet touch of his mouth competed with the silky feel of his hands as they slipped lower to glide over her exposed back, then even lower.

In a slow dance of desire, his lips moved over hers, and Chrystal instinctively pulled closer, pressing her breasts against the starched cotton of his tuxedo shirt. Her arms draped over his shoulders, her fingers seeking the warmth of his bare neck.

Tearing his mouth from hers, he finally raised his head and looked down at her, his black eyes blazing with the effort of keeping his passion in control. "Oh, God, Chrystal," he murmured, "I love you so much it hurts."

Chrystal turned dizzy with excitement—and the champange she'd drunk had nothing to do with the feeling. The success of the party, the glittering crowd below, and now, the man she'd always dreamed of—standing before her, expressing what she'd only prayed for in her dreams. She swallowed again, her heart in her throat, "I love you, too, Max."

As if the words had somehow broken the rope of restraint he'd been behind, Max crushed her to him, burying his face against her neck, his hands feverishly running up and down her back. "I've got to have you, Chrystal. Here—now."

His voice was the embodiment of her own desire, and Chrystal's world exploded. His teeth nipped lightly against her neck, and she squirmed as murmurs of passion built in her own throat.

Suddenly, even the thin barrier of gown and tuxedo seemed too much as her urgency grew to match his. She raised her hands to her neck and with nerveless fingers freed the buttons high at the neck of her gown. In a sigh of release, with a whisper of fabric, the front of the dress fell forward.

Max groaned and cupped her bare breasts with his hands, dropping the pretense of any control as Chrystal's breath came in sharply with pleasure.

"So warm," he murmured, "so soft," then his lips moved hungrily over her skin, tasting her with all the eagerness of a first time lover.

Chrystal buried her hands in his hair, her voice a needy growl. His tongue and hands moved over her with a growing need and with murmurs of support, she urged him on until he rose once more to tower over her. His eyes, as hot as his touch, raked her with heedless passion as he pulled the length of her gown up to her waist.

Dimly, she thought of the party below and the job she should be doing but as the sharp edge of her desk bit into her bare legs, Chrystal went beyond caring. The soft sound of tearing silk registered in the background of her mind as Max's fingers ripped her flimsy panties.

"Now, Chrystal, now," he urged, his voice thick with desire as he unzipped his pants. "Wrap your legs around me."

She didn't hesitate a moment, and with an abandon she'd have never thought possible, she encased his waist with first one leg and then the other, her buttocks on top of the desk. "Max," she breathed, "Oh, God . . ."

Oblivious with desire, Chrystal closed her eyes, and let her world narrow to Max and the sea of sensations washing over her. His hands, hot on her moist skin, the studs of his shirt cold against her breasts, the solid muscles beneath her legs, his lips sucking greedily against her neck—they all drew her attention momentarily before she refocused her mind and body on the hard warmth beneath her, allowing the wash of pleasure to carry her into total insensibility.

Never before had this kind of ultimate pleasure taken Chrystal so close to the edge of her endurance. Random bursts of light exploded behind her tightly closed eyelids as she felt herself carried on endless waves of satisfaction. Beneath his shirt, the smooth muscles of Max's back rippled and for one endless moment, she slipped into the blackness of passion while Max's heat throbbed within her.

The intensity that brought them together did not die slowly, and minutes passed before Chrystal realized Max had slowly trembled into stillness. She opened her eyes, the sound of their harsh breathing filling the tiny office, pulling her back into reality. His hands which had been gripping her shoulders now gradually loosened then slipped to her waist as he pulled back to look at her. Chrystal leaned back with her elbows on the white blotter, her eyes glazed, her mouth dry.

Slowly, tenderly, Max smiled, his chest still heaving but love shining from his face as he pulled her to him once more. "I love you, Chrystal," he said hoarsely. "No matter what the future brings us, don't ever forget that."

Self-consciously, Chrystal stared into the mirror near the office door, trying to see herself as the people filling her shop would. Could they tell what she'd been doing?

Would they think the blush brought to her cheeks was rouge or would they know it came from the roughness of Max's five o'clock shadow? Was the glow of happiness sparking from her eyes the result of the party's success or was it obvious that the gleam came from a much deeper source? And the tiny nips along her neck—a rash of nerves or nibbles from a hungry lover?

Behind her, Max came up and put his hands on her shoulders, answering her unspoken question. "You look perfect," he whispered, his warm breath brushing against her ear. "Don't worry. I'm the only one who knows you're not wearing any underwear." By one finger, he dangled the shredded pink silk before her face.

She laughed and snatched the panties from his hand, staring at them in mock distress. "Good grief, you're right. I guess they are past the point of wearing, aren't they?" A marvelous sense of abandonment came over her, something she'd never felt before—desirable, sexy, wanton. She turned to face him, his arms encircling her in a loose hug. "Won't everyone know though—"

He shook his head and brushed her lips with his. "Know what?" he replied. "You look absolutely gorgeous, and no one down there is going to have any idea what you've been doing up here." He grinned, a devastating smile that took her breath away. "Except for me, of course, and I'll be trying to get you back up here for the rest of the evening, believe you me."

She answered his smile with one of her own. "There's nothing I'd like better," she replied in a husky voice. She was telling the truth; she would like to stay in the office with Max or even better, slip away with him to her apartment for a more convenient, if no less exciting, replay.

"But we better get back?" Max's voice was questioning, as though he might try to talk her out of returning, but Chrystal shook her head. From her fingers, he snatched the shreds of silk she held then slipped them into his pocket.

"What do you think you're doing?"

"Hiding the evidence," he said with a grin, going to the door.

Straightening her shoulders, Chrystal smiled suggestively. "Will we need an attorney or are we co-conspirators?"

"We're more than that, baby," he said in a husky voice. "A helluva lot more."

As they entered the showroom, she expected the entire room to grow silent and stare, but nothing like that happened. The crowd was as loud and busy as ever, and they easily slipped back into the room, blending in as if they'd never been away. For the next two hours, however, every time she lifted her head, Max was there, staring at her from across the room with a tiny, knowing smile lifting his sensuous lips. Each time their eyes met, the delicious thrill of a shared secret twisted between them, making her even more anxious for Max's touch.

She tried to put aside her desire and tend to business as the party progressed smoothly. More sales were made, then a sudden murmuring, starting at the front door and moving outward, rippled through the crowd like a wave. Instantly, Max was by her side. She strained upward on her toes, leaning on his arm, trying to see to the front of the store. "What is it?" she said, her voice apprehensive. "I can't see."

"I'm not sure. There's some kind of commotion going on over by the guards."

Even as Chrystal closed her eyes and prayed, she knew something dreadful had happened. She'd been waiting all evening for catastrophe, and here it was. Dropping Max's arm, she pushed her way into the throng. The noise in the room began to subside, and the deathly quiet that precedes a disaster descended.

A corridor of expectant faces lined her way. Their greedy eyes darted from the door to her; gossip was being made. At the end of the tunnel of people, stood Neal.

His appearance registered slowly, and when it finally clicked, Chrystal's feet stumbled at the sight of her handsome brother. His once-white shirt was rumpled, and the tail hung out over the waistband of his pants. The chestnut hair he always kept shining now lie down in greasy strands, flattened over his forehead. Three days' worth of stubble darkened his cheeks: He looked like a bum who'd had a particularly hard night.

Only as she grew closer, did she see the two

policemen on either side of Neal, gripping his arms. Their appearance shocked her, but it was the sight of her brother's wrists that froze her movement. They were in handcuffs.

"Neal, what on earth is going on . . ."

"Hello, sister dearest, thought I'd drop in—brought some friends, hope you don't mind."

"Come up to my office. Now." Her voice was tight and angry.

The nearest policeman shook his head, a look of sympathy on his face. "I'm sorry, ma'am, but we're way out of line by even being here." He tilted his Stetson-covered head toward Neal. "He's a pretty convincing fellow, though, and he begged so much for us to stop, we couldn't turn him down. Told us you were his sister." The look he shared with the other policeman revealed his disbelief.

"I am." An icy fist closed around her heart as she stared at her baby brother, and she felt the calm of shock take over. "What's going on, Neal?" she said quietly.

Before Neal could answer, Max broke in. "Shall we step outside?" The reassuring warmth of his hand in the middle of her back was a welcome touch as they all trooped to the sidewalk. Behind them, the party buzzed in sudden disbelief.

She introduced them. Once, she would have been mortified for Max to see Neal like this, but now, although she was embarrassed, she wasn't disgraced.

"I'd shake your hand, but as you can see, I'm somewhat tied up at the moment," Neal sneered.

His insolence irritated Chrystal as never before. "Neal, this isn't the time to be cute. What in the hell is going on?"

His grin faded, replaced by a look of angry denial.

"Why don't you tell me? I've been on an airplane for the last twenty-four hours—which was eight hours late getting started, I might add—I get off the plane and instead of you, I find these two guys waiting for me." His little-boy face turned pouty. "You should have been at the airport to pick me up. Why weren't you there?"

"I thought you could find your own way."

"But you've always picked me up before—"

"Neal, why have you been arrested?"

"That's a really good question, but I don't have the answer. I got this letter from Max, here, and the next thing I know, I'm wearing handcuffs."

Chrystal's heart plummeted. Surely Max had nothing to do with this, but the question came out anyway as she turned to him, a sinking feeling forcing her knees to shake. "You wrote to Neal?"

"Yes, I did, Chrystal. More than two months ago, though, and all I did was tell him I thought he ought to come home and help you out of the mess he'd left you in."

Her startled glance left Max's face as the policeman on Neal's right pulled her brother's arm backwards, towards the door. "Come on, buddy, you've had a chance to see her, now we've got to go. You can explain later."

"But I—"

Chrystal put a restraining hand on the officer's arm. "Wait, please, just a few more minutes."

The other policeman stepped between them. "We've got to leave, ma'am."

"Where are you taking him?"

"Downtown. You can see him in the morning. Bring an attorney."

Chrystal followed the policemen to the sidewalk,

Max right beside her. Neal was already getting in the car. Futilely, she held her hand out to him. "Neal, I'll be there tomorrow," she cried, then added, "Max, too."

Neal stopped abruptly, half-way into the blue and white car, his look one of stubborn belligerence. Like a child whose toy has been taken away, he frowned and pursed his full lips. "Come alone," he demanded. "I don't want your fancy-boy lawyer anywhere near me."

Chrystal dropped her hand, confusion and uncertainty checking her steps. "You need an attorney, Neal. Max is my—my friend. He'll help us."

Her brother's lip curled upward in a parody of joy. "Oh, yeah, he'll help me, all right. Help me right into jail." He shook his head and climbed into the car then turned to stare at Max through the open window. "Do me a favor, Morris, and don't come. You've already done more than your share."

Neal's voice was biting, sarcastic in a way Chrystal had never heard before. Shocked, she stared first at him then at Max's impassive face. "What, what are you saying, Neal?"

The car's engine roared to life. Over the noise, she missed part of his reply, but as the automobile pulled away from the curb, "Ask your lover," floated out over the empty street. Utter stillness descended over the now-empty sidewalk. With a sickening sense of dread, Chrystal turned slowly. She didn't want to, but she knew she had to ask.

Max looked as though he'd been carved from a solid block of marble. She turned to him, and without moving a muscle, he stared back at her, his expression frozen, his eyes like black ice.

"What did Neal mean?" Her words fell like stones

to the pavement, their meaning heavy with potential destruction.

Something flickered across his face. Was it regret? Could it be disappointment? Maybe it was resignation. His sigh filled the soft night air.

"I guess Neal thinks I'm responsible for his troubles," he finally said.

Chrystal could hardly hear his words over the rush of blood through her ears and her own prayers of quiet desperation. She didn't really want to know, but the question materialized on its own. "Are you?"

He answered quickly, as if he wanted to get the words out of his mouth. "No, I'm not. No one is liable for Neal, but Neal."

Even though Chrystal agreed, a deep ache started in her chest and worked its way up. Briefly she closed her eyes against the pain, wishing the night would swallow her up. Maybe then her throat would stop burning, her struggling lungs would ease, her heart wouldn't crack into a thousand pieces.

"That's not what I meant, Max, and you know it." She ground her teeth and willed herself to stay calm, but her self-control snapped. "You were the only person I showed that telegram to. You knew he was coming in tonight. Did you call the police, Max?"

"That's what you think, isn't it? Without even giving me a chance to explain, you've accepted his word over mine."

"You just admitted you wrote to him and told him to come help me."

His voice was unyielding. "That's right. I did, and he should have."

Max's reply was all the admission she needed.

Without another thought, Chrystal raised her hand and slapped him, the sound splitting the night in two. "How could you?" she cried. "I told you I'd take care of this. You had no right to interfere."

With eyes full of obstinate rage, Max stared at her, then rubbed his jaw. "*Someone* needs to interfere with this family."

Her fury grew. "Maybe so, but who in the hell appointed you? We had an agreement, or did you conveniently forget? You said you'd leave him alone if I worked with you. Is this what you call leaving him alone?"

"Neal shouldn't be left alone, Chrystal. He needs help, serious help, can't you see that?"

"But *jail?*" Her voice rose. "Jail? My God, Max," she swung her still-stinging hand toward the store behind her, "didn't you see how humiliated he was?"

"How humiliated *he* was? What about you? What about your party? Damn it, Chrystal, he deserves to be humiliated." Max shook his head, his outrage written in deep lines across his forehead. "Frankly, I don't even see why you care."

"So he's not perfect, all right? But he's my brother, for God's sake, the only family I have left. I love him, can't you understand that? Or haven't you ever felt that emotion before?" Chrystal's chest heaved, and she brushed her hair away from her burning eyes. "Is that it? Have you been in the courtroom for so long that you can't distinguish real emotions from fake ones?"

His face knit into a fury of disbelief. "Just what in the hell does that mean?"

"Exactly what it sounded like. You play at your little legal clinic, plan grandiose centers for poor, underprivileged children and act like you're helping people but you don't ever really think about them or feel what they're feeling. You just do it because you're trying to assuage your own guilt. Their pain isn't even real to you anymore, and neither is mine.''

"You don't know what you're talking about,'' he said tightly. "I care deeply about the clinic, and yes, about your pain, but your brother's, no.''

"His problems are my problems.''

"Only because you make them, and that's the biggest mistake of your life. Don't you realize what you're doing, Chrystal? He's never going to grow up because you won't let him. When he has to face his own responsibilities, then he'll learn how to handle them.''

"Like you did in San Diego?'' she shot back.

The instant her words were out, Chrystal watched Max's face freeze, and she knew she'd scored a direct hit.

"Yes,'' he replied slowly. "Like I have.''

She'd hurt him, but the regret now building inside her chest wouldn't free her brother, and that was all Max's fault. He'd as much as admitted his part. Silence filled the deserted street and wrapped them in a blanket of misunderstanding.

Her voice was cold, and the words came out like splinters of ice, piercing her heart with pain and disappointment. "I think you better leave.''

"Yes,'' he agreed grimly. "The party's over.''

NINE

"Look at this," Marion demanded, handing Chrystal the tally from the cash register the next morning.

Chrystal raised her head from her desk and looked dully at the incredible figure. Last week, the success would have made her ecstatic; now, all she could do was look at the number and shake her head. Neal's appearance and arrest consumed her mind, yet she answered Marion with partial attention. "It's hard to believe our money problems are over that easily, isn't it?" She paused then added, "I wish everything could be solved like this."

Marion sat down beside her, dropping her high heels off with a thud. "Life isn't that simple, Chrystal, baby. I wish it was, but it's not." Marion's deep voice held a curious sadness that turned Chrystal's head. She stared at the beautiful black woman.

Marion's forehead wrinkled, and she moved closer to Chrystal, draping one arm over her shoulders. "What else happened last night, baby? You look like you're the one that got arrested instead of Neal."

Chrystal felt her bottom lip begin to quiver. "I told Max to leave." She pulled it in between her teeth in a painful attempt to halt the revealing tremble.

Marion's black eyes darkened even more. "You told Max to leave! Why, Chrystal?"

She shook her head dejectedly. "The first day he came in here, you told me about him, but I didn't listen. Gossip, I said to myself. Besides, what did I care? I was just selling him jewelry, not making some kind of commitment."

"But it turned into one anyway, didn't it?"

Chrystal nodded soundlessly, ineffectually brushing at her watery eyes. "I thought I loved him," she whispered.

"*Thought*, as in past tense?"

"Yes, as in history, over, kaput." She straightened in the chair, her back a steel rod. "I'll never forgive him for what he did to Neal."

Marion's mouth fell open, her dark, red lips parting with an audible gasp. "You broke off with Max because Neal was arrested? Why?"

Chrystal felt her irritation grow. "Haven't you been listening to a word I said, Marion? Max wrote Neal months ago and told him to come home. We had an agreement that he'd leave Neal alone but he broke it."

"Max wrote Neal?" she said faintly.

"Yes, and besides that, Max knew Neal was coming. I made the mistake of showing him a telegram that Neal sent me last week." She swallowed hard, a cold knot in her stomach. "Max told the police, and they were waiting for Neal when he got off the plane."

Marion's voice rose in shock and disbelief. "Did Max admit that?"

Chrystal held back her tears with a sniff. "He didn't have to. Neal told me."

"Neal told you." Marion repeated the words with perplexity. "'How'd he have time to tell you all this? He was only here a second."

"That was long enough, believe me."

"Enough to give up on the man you love?"

Chrystal's jaw twitched, and she angrily flipped her bangs away from her forehead. "Yes."

"Just like that." Marion snapped her fingers, a loud pop. "You're going to make a decision that could affect the rest of your life? You, Miss Chrystal-I'll-think-about-it-forever?" She shook her head, the heavy, black braids swinging back and forth like angry snakes.

Chrystal's smoldering anger flamed. "Yes, damnit, just like that." She snapped her own fingers under Marion's nose. "That's all Max gave our agreement. One second of thought, then boom! He went after my brother like the barracuda I knew he was." She stood up, her rage too intense to sit still any longer. "We had an agreement, Marion. He was supposed to leave Neal alone if I cooperated, which I did. Max betrayed me, and I'll never forgive him."

Marion's face turned hard, and she crossed her own arms with a look of disgust. "How come you can make excuses for Neal till the cows come home, but you aren't even reasonable about Max? Huh? Tell me that."

Her vehemence startled Chrystal. "I am being reasonable; he's the traitor."

Like a cannon, Marion shot to her feet. Her nose was inches from Chrystal's "Nobody's a traitor, here. We're only trying to do the right thing. Max is a good man, Chrystal. In fact, he's the best thing that ever happened to you, and you're going to dump him just because of that rotten brother of yours. For years Neal has manipulated you, abused you, and taken advantage of you, but Maxwell Morris made you happy, don't you realize that? Or has it been so long that you forgot what that feeling was called? Why, you were practically walking on air last night before Neal came.''

Chrystal felt her eyes widen, and Marion's vigorous nodding confirmed it. "Oh, yeah, I saw it. Stevie Wonder would have. Don't you realize you and Max are . . . are, well, connected somehow.'' Her gold earrings trembled and swung as she nodded. "I don't know, but it's like there's some kind of chain that joins you. From the first day that man walked in here, I saw it. Why can't you?''

Chrystal felt her heart crack. Her eyes filled with tears, but she blinked them back. "I can," she whispered, "but it's too late, Marion.''

The day crawled by, an incredible sadness covering her like an old blanket. Numbly, Chrystal went through the motions of work, waiting for six o'clock. She'd told Neal she'd come to the jail and try to arrange bail after closing the shop.

I'd like to leave him there a few days. As soon as the thought came, it disappeared, but not without her wondering where it came from. She should feel sorry for him; she should be anxious to see him; she should go take care of him. Shouldn't she?

An hour later, she was on the freeway. The closer she got to the downtown jail, the more anxious she felt. How was she going to get him out of this? Her thoughts automatically turned to Max, and she found herself wishing for him before she remembered.

She relived the scene on the sidewalk last night: Max's dark, brooding face came to her mind, and a small sob escaped. *Damnit!* Neal wouldn't even be in jail if it weren't for Max!

She'd trusted him, and this was what she'd gotten. *Hell,* she chastised herself, *let's tell the truth. You loved the son-of-a—*

The city facility loomed to her left, and she exited the freeway then pulled into the parking lot. Her fingers shook as she turned off the ignition, and for two seconds, she rested her head on the steering wheel. Three deep breaths finally slowed her racing heart, but when she lifted her eyes and stared at the brick building before her, she was not any calmer.

The stark outlines of the building wavered as she stared at the red brick with tearful eyes. Somewhere behind one of those tiny windows her baby brother sat, waiting for her. Waiting for her to make it right, to fix it, like she always had.

Her knees were shaking when she approached the reception desk minutes later and asked for directions, but the uniformed woman behind the Formica expanse never looked up from her computer, just pointed to a room down the hall. Chrystal soon found herself in a larger room that looked like a doctor's waiting office. The tiny, dark booths she'd imagined, with grilled partitions and telephones, were nowhere in sight.

What did fill the room were people. White people, black people, brown, yellow, and everything in between. Young, old, babies, grandfathers, mothers, they were all there, and they were all talking at once. The din was overwhelming.

As she waited for Neal, Chrystal studied the family closest to her.

They weren't unusual; they didn't look any different from any others, but as Chrystal watched them, the crack in her heart, started last night when Neal had first appeared in handcuffs, opened a little more.

From her plastic chair, a tired-looking woman leaned forward and spoke, but the teenager across from her ignored her pleas. Instead, he stared insolently at Chrystal. Two smaller children clung to the woman's knees, begging for attention and fussing at each other. Chrystal tried not to listen, but snatches of the conversation drifted to her.

"Johnny, I know the other kids made you do it, but I can't convince your father. He says you're going to have to stay here this time."

This pronouncement caught his attention, and his head swiveled, Chrystal obviously forgotten. "Hell, no. You can forget that crap about me staying here. You've got to get me out of here. You promised," he said in an accusatory tone.

"Yes, sweetheart, I know I did, and believe me, I'm doing all I can, but this *is* your third arrest, and the bail has been set higher this time." Without missing a beat, she separated the fighting children at her feet. "I've missed a lot of work trying to talk to the judge, but he's really busy, and I just don't know . . ."

"Listen, I wouldn't even be here if it wasn't for you, and you know it. If you'd given me the money like I asked for, I wouldn't have even gone with Doug that night, but no, you couldn't even fork over twenty bucks. What did you expect me to do? Go out with the guys and not have any money?" He sniffed angrily and flicked his eyes in Chrystal's direction.

She immediately looked down at her lap, but not before their eyes met. The insolence and disrespect in his stare shocked her. Didn't he realize his mother was trying to help him? Why was he ignoring her? His obnoxious demeanor was more than Chrystal could bear, but before she could get up and move, Neal walked up.

He'd replaced the rumpled clothes of the night before with drab overalls, but he hadn't shaved or combed his hair. The handcuffs were gone, and on his feet he wore open-ended sandals. They were too big, and he had to shuffle to keep them on as he sat down in the chair beside her.

Chrystal blinked and stared at her brother, then on their own volition her eyes darted back to the nearby teenager. Now he was bent closer to his mother in an apparent change of tactics. He held her hand and was smiling engagingly, his voice low and persuasive. She was nodding. He must have felt Chrystal's gaze because he lifted his face and looked directly at her then winked.

She stared at him coldly. On the inside, she screamed silently at the woman's slightly curved back. *Don't you see what he's doing? How can you be so blind?* The woman, of course, didn't hear her. Chrystal had the feeling, though, that even if she'd raged out loud, the mother wouldn't have listened— just as she never had about Neal.

"Hey, did you come to see them or me?" Neal broke in petulantly.

Chrystal pulled her gaze away from the teenager, surveyed the room then finally spoke, ignoring Neal's question. Her voice was slow, and her words were deliberate. "I am tired," she said. "I am sick and tired . . . of taking care of you."

Abruptly, he dropped her hand and pulled back, a look of utter shock on his face. "What, what do you mean?"

"Exactly what I said, Neal. I've just had a revelation, and if you want to thank someone, you can talk to that young man over there." She pointed to the blond teenager who was walking his mother to the door, his arm around her shoulders.

"Do you know him?" Neal asked, his voice puzzled.

"Yes," she said sadly. "That's you, ten years ago."

"You're crazy." He jumped up and towered over her. "I was never in jail when I was that young."

"Yes, that's right. I always bailed you out before it got that far, didn't I?"

His jaw tightened. Chrystal had never seen the glint that suddenly appeared in his dark blue eyes. He obviously didn't know what to say, and his gaze darted back to the departing teen as though seeking an explanation to Chrystal's startling actions.

He sat back down beside her, clearly puzzled but unmistakably ready to try to change her mind. Moving closer, with an air of concern, he draped one arm around her shoulder then leaned over and kissed her cheek. "Look, Chrys, you're obviously under a great deal of strain, and I haven't helped any, I know." He pulled his lips in, making small sounds of regret and shaking his head. "Why don't you come back tomorrow, and we can talk then. I don't mind staying here another day." With a skill that Robert Redford would admire, he hung his head. "Hell, I deserve it, I know. You go on home, baby. Get me a good lawyer, and come back tomorrow.''

"I've got a good lawyer, Neal, but I won't be coming back tomorrow.''

The little-boy smile stayed on his face despite her words. "Sure you will, Chrys. I need your help to get out of here.''

"I know you do, but this time, you won't be getting it.''

His expression suddenly changed. "You aren't mad at me about the bills I left you with, are you? I meant to pay everyone, I really did. I can explain all that, Chrys, I promise.''

She smiled evenly. "No, that's not necessary.''

"Well, what is it then?'' he demanded. "You want a piece of me, too, just like everyone else? Like that flashy lawyer boyfriend of yours? I knew when I got that letter that he was going to be trouble.'' Neal stood again, this time his agitation revealed as he forced his hands through his hair. He paced in front of Chrystal with feverish energy. "He said I'd left you in the lurch and if I loved you at all, I should come home and help you, but hell, I knew you could handle it. Right?''

"Right,'' she repeated faintly.

"Yeah, that's what I thought, so I just ignored the letter. I knew you'd be okay, but then I wrote you, guess you didn't get it, the mail from Jakarta's pretty bad, and when I didn't hear from you, I didn't know what else to do but come home.'' He continued to walk back and forth. "The guys I was dealing with over there are pretty rough, and when my cash got short—well, I had to come up with some rubles or leave. I came home to get some money from you and when I got off the plane, the damn cops were standing there.''

He paused briefly then in a voice of gentle reproach, he continued. ''If you'd sent me the money I asked for in the letter, I wouldn't have gotten arrested, Chrystal.''

The crack in her heart opened wider, and Chrystal felt torn in two. Part of her wanted to console him, the other part wanted to shake him. For two seconds, she was torn, then she stood up, her shoulders back, her spine steel. ''Neal, this is probably going to come as a shock to you, but I got your letter. I chose not to send you the money—''

''You got my letter? My God, Chrystal, why didn't you wire me the cash?'' His voice rose in disbelief, and his face began to flush. ''I can't believe this. You actually knew I was in trouble and didn't bother to help me out? How could you be so heartless? Don't you think of anyone but yourself?''

The cool façade she'd been hiding behind fissured, but she held onto the edges of her control. ''How can you ask me that, Neal? I've been there for you every step of the way.''

''Well, I think that's pretty debatable right now, sister dearest.''

Disbelief flushed her face. ''Neal, I nearly lost the store, and everything else I own, because of those bills you left me. Did you think about that before you took off?''

''Hey, you're making this sound like it's all my fault. Where do you come off doing that? You've never talked to me like this before.'' His face turned suspicious. ''Is all this your fancy boyfriend's idea? Are you sleeping with that guy?''

Chrystal's spine straightened, and staring at him

with eyes like glaciers, and a voice to match, she answered, "That is none of your business, but I will tell you that Max has nothing to do with my decision. You're the one that opened my eyes, you and this place and the people in it." She grabbed her purse from the plastic chair and took a deep breath. "The only injustice I ever did you was not making you responsible for yourself. I loved you too much, that's my only crime."

She turned to leave. Neal stood dumbly then raced to her side as she reached the door. He jumped in front of her and put his hand on the door. "Wait," he pleaded. "You can't leave me in here, Chrystal. This place is a zoo. I've got to get out."

She looked him straight in the eye, her answer as hard as the diamonds in her store. "That's your problem."

Chrystal sat in the darkened living room of her condo and stared at the blackness. She felt invisible. Empty and invisible. Neal's pleas still rang in her ears, and she involuntarily put her hands up as if she could stop the sound. But the cries were from inside her head, and she dropped her hands, knowing there was no way she could turn them off.

As if Neal's voice wasn't enough, Max's face filled her vision. She remembered how he looked after her poisonous words; his dark eyes had been raw with hurt, hurt she'd put there. Then she remembered how, only hours before, he'd gazed at her with desire and told her how much he loved her. She covered her face, silent sobs shaking her slim shoulders. He'd never forgive her.

She couldn't forgive herself.

But why should she? A self-righteous indignation

swept over her in the darkness of the room. Max was the one that brought all this down on them. If he'd stuck to their agreement and left Neal alone, then sooner or later fate would have caught up with him. No, Max had betrayed her trust, and she'd never be able to forgive him. A relationship without that foundation would never survive.

She rose abruptly, as if by moving she'd be able to escape her thoughts and went into the kitchen, automatically filling the coffee grinder with fresh beans. She might as well make coffee; there would be no sleep for her tonight.

TEN

Max stared blindly at the coffee cup he cradled in his hands. In his mind, thoughts of Chrystal burned as hotly as the china between his blunt fingers. He lifted the mug to his lips and took a sip of the steaming liquid then cursed soundly as the coffee scalded his lips and tongue.

On second thought, he welcomed the pain; at least the throbbing burn was a feeling—one to replace the emptiness he'd felt since leaving Chrystal. When she'd told him to leave, after all they'd shared, his heart had fallen to the sidewalk, and he had yet to recover. He'd been numb ever since.

Only a few days had passed since the party but they were long ones, and the nights even longer. The void Chrystal's absence produced was unlike anything Max had ever experienced, and the feeling was not one he wanted to prolong.

Hooking his thumb in the handle of the mug, Max leaned back and swiveled his leather chair until he could stare out the windows behind his desk. He brought the coffee cup back to his mouth and blew on the still-steaming brew.

How to proceed? The question had haunted him ever since he'd stormed off that night, and the answer was no closer now. Chrystal was so blind to her brother's faults that Max felt there was no way they could ever reconcile.

Even if they could make peace between them, would he ever be able to forget her mindless acceptance of Neal's condemnation? She'd been angry, and he could forgive her words spoken in fury, but the way she'd heedlessly taken Neal's indictment was more than Max could bear. He grimaced; the painful memory was still a fresh and open wound.

A cold feeling settled over him, despite the hot coffee. Feeling drained and just as hollow as the cup in his hand, he leaned forward and set the empty mug on the credenza before him. Chrystal was gone, out of his life for good; she'd made her choice perfectly clear. He'd just have to accept that fact and go on. The invisible bond he'd always felt they shared was just that; invisible because it was nonexistent. He shook his head, his face a grim mask as he turned back to his desk.

Work had healed his hurt before; maybe it would this time, too.

During the week following the party, a steady stream of customers kept Chrystal and Marion busy. Even at Christmas, Cummins hadn't had this many sales. The party had definitely brought the store back to life.

On Saturday, Chrystal finally locked the doors at eight, two hours later than usual, and retreated to her office. Marion was waiting for her.

"You're still here?" Chrystal glanced at the black woman then pulled off her shoes and rubbed her weary feet. "I thought you'd left after you finished with Mrs. Finklestein."

Marion nervously twirled one gold loop in her ear. "Yes, I was going to, but then, I thought, well—"

If she hadn't known the woman for twenty years, Chrystal would have sworn the salesclerk wore a guilty look. "What is it?"

Marion cleared her throat, checked her earrings again, then glanced out the window as if searching for the right words in the soft, summer night. Finally, she answered Chrystal's question with one of her own. "Did you go back to see Neal again?"

Chrystal released the breath she'd been holding; she'd had the most terrible feeling that Marion had more bad news. All she wanted was to know about Neal? "No. Once was more than enough. You were right."

Marion's hand flew to the neckline of her dress. "Right? Right about what?"

Chrystal threw down the high heel she'd been clutching and leaned back into her chair, her back slumping against the padded cushion. "Oh, hell, Marion, right about everything. Right about Neal, right about Max, right about me." Her voice turned hard. "I should have listened to you."

"I'm not so sure about that."

Chrystal shook her head. "No, don't act modest. You *were* right. I didn't know how to love Neal, and I've managed to really mess things up. He's in jail, Max hates me, and the one thing I thought I wanted most—a successful store—seems pointless now because I lost everything else. Where did I go wrong?"

Marion cleared her throat. "I don't know about you, Chrystal, but I do know where I went wrong, and it's time I try to fix it."

An instant of affection washed over Chrystal. "Oh, Marion, this isn't your problem, and you can't fix it, no matter how hard you try." She reached over and patted the woman's silk-covered knee. "You've been very helpful."

"That's not true." Marion's voice cracked, and Chrystal's foreboding returned in full force. "I haven't been helpful, I've been meddling and poking my nose where I shouldn't have, and now you've lost the best chance at happiness you've ever had, just because of me."

She bent her head and started to cry. Chrystal was instantly shocked into silence. In all the years she'd known Marion, she'd never seen the dignified black woman break down and cry.

"Marion, what on earth are you talking about?"

Her face looked like onyx with diamonds sprinkled down it; teardrops glistened in the deepening gloom of the office. "Max didn't turn Neal in, Chrystal. I did."

Chrystal stared dumbly at Marion and blinked. Inside her chest, her heart began to thud. The thumping seemed to keep pace with the words echoing in her mind. "No (beat, beat), no (beat, beat)." Finally she found her voice and with careful precision she spoke. "Exactly what are you saying, Marion?"

She sniffed then rubbed her hand across her forehead. "Two weeks ago, the Los Angeles police department called looking for Neal. They knew he'd left Jakarta and was coming here. Apparently the authorities over there were already searching for him.'' Chrystal watched the column of Marion's throat move as she swallowed hard. "I saw the telegram he sent you; I told the police which plane he'd be on.''

Instantly, Chrystal's world tilted on its axis, and she gripped the edge of the desk to stop the spinning. An overwhelming dizziness forced her eyes closed, but when she opened them, nothing had changed, and she actually felt ill. All the hateful things she'd said to Max, all the pain she'd caused him, all for nothing? The unjustness of it all . . .

For two seconds, Marion averted her eyes and stared at the floor. A flash of defiance lit her face as she raised it once more. "Neal did wrong; he deserves to pay for it.''

Chrystal wanted to lash out and hurt Marion just as she'd hurt Max. She slapped the top of the desk with the flat of her hand, and the angry sound filled the tiny room. "Yes, Neal deserves to pay for his mistakes, but I don't. Do you realize what you did? Marion, I sent Max away because I thought he turned Neal in. I said cruel and hateful things. Things Max will never be able to forgive.''

Marion's forehead wrinkled into chocolate lines of sympathy and regret. "But I had no idea you'd blame Max, or I'd never have done it, Chrystal, I swear.'' She hung her head again.

The dejection on the normally serene woman's face erased the flash of Chrystal's anger. How could she be mad at Marion; she'd been the mother Chrystal had never had. Chrystal felt her shoulders slump. "Oh, Marion, you did what you thought was right at the time. I understand, believe me.''

She watched the heavy braids move as Marion shook her head and raised her face once more. "But

I hurt you. I never meant to do that, baby. I just wanted to help, I didn't mean to do anything wrong." Her eyes were red, and they overflowed once more.

Chrystal stood and moved to the window at the back of her office. The inky blackness outside mirrored the darkness she felt in her heart. "The only person that's been wrong in this whole event is me. I was too blind to see what you and Max tried to point out, and then I compounded the mistake by unfairly accusing Max. Even if he *had* turned in Neal, I shouldn't have exploded like I did. You were both right, but I was too stubborn to see it."

Marion sniffled behind her. "You weren't stubborn; you were in love."

Chrystal stared at her wavering reflection in the glass. A crushing sadness overwhelmed her, a loss so great she could hardly bear to acknowledge it. She struggled to keep her voice steady. "Call the feeling what you want, it's gone now, that's for sure."

In the glass, she watched the black woman rise then come up behind her. Marion's broad hands covered Chrystal's shoulders, and like two ghosts, their eyes met and merged in the wavering image mirrored in the window. "It doesn't have to be over. Go to him, Chrystal. Tell him that you love him."

In the ashes of Chrystal's hope, a spark of unbidden love flamed then died. "He wouldn't even let me in his office, Marion. I said some pretty nasty things to him."

"Do you love him?"

"Desperately."

"Does he love you?"

He'd told her that he did. Once he'd begged for a

chance to prove it, but now? She shook her head. "I'm not sure any more."

Marion's fingers gripped her shoulders tightly. "There's only one way to find out, isn't there?"

Max's office looked exactly like Chrystal had thought it would when she arrived the next day. Vast couches of butter-soft leather circled a glass-topped cocktail table, while on the wall, contemporary prints of bright, splashy colors pulled the eye upward. The waiting receptionist pulled the eye back.

"May I help you?" the stunning blonde inquired as she surveyed Chrystal's simple white suit with a critical stare.

Chrystal tightened her grip on the single white rose she carried and aimed a steady look back. Her voice was low and cool. "I'm here to see Max."

The blonde dropped her azure eyes to the desk calendar before her. "Do you have an appointment, Miss—"

"No, but he'll see me."

"He's very busy today. In fact, he's in meetings all day. If you'd like to leave your name, perhaps . . ."

A snotty secretary wasn't going to deter her now; this meant to much. Never lowering her head, Chrystal leaned forward and rested her hands on the desk. Her knees were shaking, but her voice was like steel. "Please tell Max that Chrystal is here. He will see me."

A look of righteous indignation crossed the secretary's face, but it was quickly followed by a flicker of uncertainty. Chrystal smiled politely; the secretary rose. "Just a moment," she snapped.

The woman disappeared through a heavy wooden

door behind her desk as Chrystal straightened up. She seemed unable to loosen the tight grip she kept on the rose in her hand, and suddenly, she started to lay it down on the couch. Why in the world had she stopped to pick it up? Had she thought Max might change his mind if she showed up with a flower, for God's sake? She had an insane urge to run out the door, leaving an empty office behind. But she didn't. She took a deep breath and waited nervously.

When the door opened again, Chrystal turned expectantly, but instead of Max, the now-smug blonde stood demurely by her desk. She could barely conceal her delight. "Mr. Morris is busy, but if you'd like to wait . . ." Her attitude finished the sentence even though her words had stopped. *You can—till hell freezes over.*

Chrystal's disappointment rose in the back of her throat with an aching pain, but she smiled blandly and took a seat exactly opposite the blonde's desk. "Fine."

Before she could even put her purse down, the door behind the secretary's desk opened, and Max emerged. He brushed past the blonde, whose vermilion mouth now hung open, and walked stiffly to Chrystal.

Her shock at his sudden appearance turned into a storm of emotions. Delight, anger, sadness, and finally, longing all washed over her.

He wore a pair of faded jeans and a black cotton sweater, and Chrystal's lungs felt suddenly constricted. The jeans were obviously favorites, soft and old, and he looked incredibly confident in the elegant surroundings and comfortable clothing. The blood coursed through her veins at an uncomfortable rate as she remembered what he looked like underneath.

She opened her mouth but nothing came out. He rescued her. "Please come in, Chrystal. My phone call finished quicker than Eva thought it would."

The blonde stared daggers at Chrystal as she and Max walked past her into his office. The door closed behind them, and Chrystal smiled at Max. "I don't think Eva likes me."

His own smile was forced. "Don't worry about her; she treats everyone that way. She sees herself as my personal guardian."

Mentally, Chrystal compared Eva to Marion. Salt and pepper. She raised her eyebrows at Max. "How interesting. Why does everyone seem to think that you and I need protecting?"

Max stared at her strangely, but she ignored his look and walked into the huge office. Before the bank of glass that covered one wall, a giant partners desk rested. Two wing-backed chairs covered in tapestry waited to one side. To the left, a small grouping of chairs and a low divan surrounded a butlers table, the top of which was covered by a silver coffee service.

Now, it was Chrystal's turn to look at Max with curiosity. "I didn't know you were into antiques."

"There's a lot about me you don't know, Chrystal."

She'd been staring at the beautiful furniture, but his accusation jerked her gaze back to his face. When she saw his eyes, she realized he wasn't going to make this easy. She didn't know what to say; he was right. She'd judged, condemned, and hung him without a trial.

He walked to where she stood, close enough for her to see the flecks of pain in his black eyes. "Would you like some coffee?" he asked.

"No, thank you."

The clean smell of the French soap he favored drifted to her, and the urge to smooth the frown from his face made her hand twitch. Mechanically, she gripped the rose in her hand even tighter.

He looked like he wanted to say something else, but "Shall we sit down?" came out instead. She nodded soundlessly and followed his outstretched hand to the divan. She wanted him to sit beside her, but he didn't. Instead, he took one of the generous arm chairs in front of the sofa, and her disappointment, tangled up with hope, contrition, and love, knotted in her chest like a giant ball of yarn.

If she hadn't felt the snarl of emotions coursing through her at the sight of him, Chrystal might have thought he was a stranger. The black eyes that had once stared at her with passion now glittered like cold shards of onyx. The strong fingers gripping the wooden handle of the silver coffee pot had caressed her with tenderness; now the knuckles were white with tension as he poured his coffee. And that mouth, the mouth that had once pressed so lovingly against her own, now it was compressed into a slash of animosity.

He picked up the china mug and sat back into the chair. The delicate cup trembled once before he wrapped both of his hands around it.

"Who's your guardian?" he asked abruptly.

He sounded angry, almost jealous, she thought with a start, but she forced herself to be realistic. His attitude made his position abundantly clear; Maxwell Morris wished her out of his office and out of his life—permanently. He didn't really care who her protector was.

She drew a deep breath. She would apologize for her beastly behavior then leave. Any attempts at a reconciliation were hopeless. Heartache joined the knot in her chest, but she forced herself to match his coolness and answered his question. "Marion, I'm afraid."

The angry seam of his mouth softened a fraction. "Marion?" Looking thoughtful, he paused a moment then answered. "Yes, I guess I can see that. What did she do?"

Chrystal swallowed, suddenly wishing she'd accepted the coffee. At least then her mouth wouldn't feel so dry. Her hands, though, seemed to be trying to compensate; they were dripping wet. She searched for the right words.

He sat across the gleaming silver from her and broke her already cracked heart with his stare. "Well? What's she done?" he repeated.

"She did what I accused you of: She turned in Neal." The words came out in a rush then lay between them like something someone had forgotten to hide when company came.

His face didn't change. Not one iota, not one twitch. A long silence stretched. "Good" was all he finally said.

Irritation welled in Chrystal's heart, but quickly subsided. He had every right. She glanced down at her tightly clutched hands then raised her eyes to his face once more. "I owe you an apology, Max. That's what I came here for. I'm sorry, I was wrong. Wrong about a lot of things, I guess."

Was that a flicker of understanding in his dark eyes or just a blink? She continued, "Marion told me yesterday that the police had called, looking for Neal, and she told them when his plane was coming in. I don't even know if Neal knows or not. And frankly I no longer care. It took me a long time, but

I have to admit, I'm finally seeing the person he really is and frankly I don't care for what I see."

This time, Max's jaw moved slightly, as if he were thawing a bit. "Did he go back to Indonesia?"

"Hardly. He's still in jail."

The hot coffee jiggled in the china cup, and she watched with fascination until Max finally got it back under control. He looked up, his dark eyebrows arched like two inverted V's over his black eyes. "You didn't bail him out?"

"No, I didn't, and I don't plan on doing so, either. Marion went to see him, though. She said he'd been assigned a public defender and had started counseling with the jail's psychologist."

He'd tilted forward in his chair during their conversation but now, he leaned back as though he needed more room to absorb her surprising information. He sipped his coffee.

As he pressed his lips against the rim, she found herself envious of the china mug. She broke her stare. "I didn't come here to talk about Neal, Max. I just wanted to let you know that I'm sorry for the way things turned out. I was mad that night, and I said some pretty awful things, things I didn't really mean." She rose from her chair and prepared to leave. There was nothing left to say.

He stood up abruptly. "Words of anger are usually pretty truthful."

For a long second, Chrystal held his stony gaze, but misery overwhelmed her at his look. She swirled and faced the windows, a finger under one eye to stem the flow of tears. "No, they're not. Painful, maybe, truthful, no. I accused you of running away from your responsibilities and that's the farthest thing from the truth there is."

He came up behind her, so close that she could hear him breathing. His voice was harsh. "What do you mean?"

"You left San Diego, but you didn't leave your mistakes. You carried them with you, examined them, then did something productive with your pain—the clinic and the child care center."

He brushed past her, his sleeve touching hers, and she felt as though she'd stepped too close to a blaze. If he noticed, he didn't acknowledge it, but continued until reaching the massive desk. He turned to face her once more, leaning one hip casually against the corner of the wooden antique.

"That's not what you said last week."

"I know."

"You said I was running away from my problems, not facing them."

"I know."

"You said I interfered, called me a traitor."

Max's image wavered as her eyes filled with burning tears, and her throat ached. "I know," she cried, "and I'm sorry, all right? I was wrong. What else do you want from me?"

He took two steps toward her, stopped, then reached out and pulled her roughly to his chest. With punishing force, he ground his lips against hers, the sharp edge of his teeth biting into her mouth. Like an animal in pain, a low moan came from deep within his chest.

Chrystal's mind went blank, but her body responded. Her arms snaked around his neck, and her hands pressed the back of his head in an effort to deepen the kiss. The blood screamed in her ears as her pulse raced to keep up with her pounding heart.

His kiss communicated a desperation she'd never

experienced before, and the tortured press of his lips against hers said what he wouldn't. Heat radiated down her back where his hands clutched her shoulders, and the smell of his skin filled her mind with images she'd thought she'd banished. Of their own volition, her fingers curled in his silky hair until his agonized murmur grew deeper.

Finally, he tore his mouth from hers, and with an abruptness that sent her reeling, he dropped his arms from her shoulders. She stumbled backwards, the salty taste of blood on her tongue making her realize she'd bit the inside of her lip.

The sound of his harsh breathing filled the office. Chrystal stared at him, her fingers touching her bruised and reddened lips, her chest heaving.

"That's what I want from you, Chrystal. That and much, much more. But you can't give me everything I need. You told me that yourself."

"But things have changed. I understand now what I didn't then."

"It's too late. You chose loyalty to your past, not your future. How could I ever be sure you wouldn't do the same again?"

"I didn't know how to love, Max, and if you don't know how to love, you don't know how to trust. I thought you had betrayed me. You would have felt the same."

"No," he said vehemently. "Never. I would have trusted you, but I can't now."

There was nothing more to say. She stared at him, knowing her eyes were wide and filled with tears, then she turned and left.

Only after she reached her car did she realize she still clutched the rose. Slowly, reluctantly, she opened her fist and let the bud fall gently to the pavement at her feet. At the tip of her ring finger, glistening like a tiny ruby, a single drop of blood welled.

ELEVEN

Afterwards, Chrystal wondered how she'd gotten home. She didn't remember leaving Max's office or even the drive home. In fact, the feeling of numbness haunted her for days.

Every morning she rose and went to work. Every evening she closed the store and came home. When thoughts of Max entered her mind, she would shut her brain off and refuse to acknowledge them; they were simply too painful.

But every time the bell tinkled above the store's door, she found herself stopping to see who had entered, even if she had another customer. When the phone rang, she raced to pick up the receiver, and if a long, black car pulled up to the curb, her hands would grow damp before she would see that it wasn't a Mercedes.

Finally she began to realize that Max wasn't coming back. The kiss they'd shared had been their last, and his words hadn't been necessary to explain why. She felt like she'd lost her future.

In contrast, her business was doing fantastic. The party had spread the word; apparently, even Neal's appearance had added to the mystique. Every day, more and more customers came into the tiny shop, and Chrystal had more special orders than she had time to design.

She was sitting at Marion's desk, sketching a new ring for Mrs. Smythe when the door opened, and Mrs. Meriweather, in her customary haze of Joy, entered the shop, Little Bit strolling slowly behind her, intent on preserving his dignity.

Chrystal immediately dropped her pen and greeted them. "Why, hello, how are you two?" She bent down and scratched the tiny dog's head. He looked at her with droopy eyes, then shook his ears as though he had better things to do.

In contrast, Mrs. Meriweather beamed, her large bosom heaving expectantly, her black eyes snapping. "Oh, Chrystal, I just came from the child care center that Max and I opened, and it's so wonderful I can't tell you. I feel like I've gotten a new start on life. I haven't been this excited since I don't know when."

Chrystal felt her smile fade, but before she could stop the words, they jumped out of her mouth. "Was Max there?"

The tiny French chair before the counter groaned as the sturdy matron sat down, Little Bit leaping to her lap before she was even settled. He hopped about the generous expanse of her silk dress then finally flopped down as if exhausted by the exercise of getting comfortable, his tiny, pink tongue hanging out. Two seconds later, his eyes instantly shut, and he started to snore lightly.

"Well, of course, he was there, you silly girl. He looked positively ravishing, I might add. Can men

look ravishing? Well, I guess so, he certainly did.''
She shook her head, as if in disbelief. ''That clinic
is a godsend. Why, those poor, little children. Some
of them were staying in homeless shelters. Can you
believe that? Their parents couldn't get jobs because
they had no place to put the children while they
worked. Max solved that problem, though. He's
quite a man, I must admit.''

Chrystal nodded her agreement and hid the pain
that blossomed in her heart like a blood red poppy.
It was a physical ache, and when she realized what
she was doing, she dropped the fist she'd been pressing to her breast.

''Well, anyway, we didn't come by to discuss
Max, did we, baby?'' Mrs. Meriweather yanked Little Bit up and held him in front of her face, cooing
and smiling at the now grumpy dog. She shook him
slightly. ''Wake up, sleepy head. You can't go to
beddie-bye now.''

In a half-hearted attempt at ferociousness, the dog
growled lightly and lifted his upper lip, revealing one
long incisor. Mrs. Meriweather laughed and shook
him again. ''Oh, you silly thing, are you trying to
scare Mommie?''

With little ceremony, she plopped the dog down
at her feet and turned to business. ''I want you to
design a special pin, Chrystal, that I can give to
all the workers at the child care clinic. Something
contemporary. Talk to Max about it, I'm sure he'll
have some ideas.''

Before Chrystal could argue, Mrs. Meriweather
rose. ''Do you know this woman in San Diego he
named the center after?''

The abrupt switch in conversation threw Chrystal.
''Woman in San Diego?''

"Yes, I believe he said her name was Tia Sanchez."

Chrystal recognized the name. She was the woman who had been killed by the man Max had gotten acquitted. She shook her head. "No, I never knew her."

Mrs. Meriweather nodded her gray helmet of hair. "I assumed she was dead by something he said, but I didn't want to ask. What do you think—"

Mrs. Meriweather's words were interrupted by the soft jingling of the bells above the door. Little Bit barked joyfully, jumped from her lap, and ran to the front of the store, excitedly circling the long legs of the man who had entered. Max smiled evenly then bent down and patted the tiny dog.

Chrystal's throat went dry. When Mrs. Meriweather glanced at her slyly and said her goodbyes, all Chrystal could do was nod silently. The stout matron sailed up to Max, kissed him soundly on the mouth, then navigated out the door, Little Bit tugging at the leash and barking an angry protest as though he'd rather stay and see what Max was doing there.

The store fell into an expectant silence.

Chrystal waited behind the counter as he approached. As if in a dream, she watched him raise his hand. He held out a single calla lily.

She looked down at the aristocratic flower and blinked, willing the moisture in her eyes to stay put. The long, green stem curved gracefully, and the single flower at the top was perfectly white. It held no fragrance.

"For old times' sake?" she asked quietly.

An answer must have seemed superfluous to him

because he simply smiled gently and put it into her hand, moving to a nearby case without a word.

Only a few weeks had passed but she suddenly felt as though she'd been robbed of a lifetime. His hair was longer than ever, but slicked back neatly. He looked exactly like he had months ago when he'd first walked into her store, but in her heart, she knew better. The custom-made suit, the hand-sewn shoes, the white linen handkerchief she knew he carried in his inside right coat pocket—they were all accoutrements. The trappings of his lifestyle, nothing more, nothing less. And she loved him for them because they told her he *was* a real person, in need of props like everyone else.

Her heartbeat grew erratic as he silently perused the display of sparkling gems. Finally he lifted his head and walked straight to her, his decision apparently made.

His eyes met hers and held them with a silent message she couldn't receive. *I'm miserable, and I came in here to tell you that I love you. I can't live without you and if that means putting up with this insane loyalty you have for your brother then I'll do it—as long as I get the same kind of allegiance.* "How are you?"

She met his stare and answered. "Fine."*I'm horrible. I can't sleep, I can't eat, all I do is think about you and wonder what you're doing. In my mind, I replay the horrible scene from the sidewalk a hundred times a day and curse myself again for telling you to leave. It was the most stupid thing I've ever done in my life.*

"The shop looks great. I hear business is booming."

"Yes, it is. Did Hiram tell you that?"

Max grinned. "Yeah. He told me he tried to buy

you out, but you wouldn't have anything to do with him."

"That's true. I couldn't believe it when he came in here last week. I paid him off, and he acted like he was doing *me* a favor."

Max nodded then cleared his throat. "Yes, well, speaking of hard to believe, I'm here on business."

Alarm jumped into her chest with a single leap. "Oh, no, Max, I paid all those debts—"

He held up one broad hand as if to stop her words. "No, no," he said, and Chrystal's pulse slowed slightly. "I want to buy something."

His words twisted her heart in a tiny dance of pain. If things had only turned out differently . . . She smiled politely, but the back of her throat burned. "Sure," she said hoarsely. "What can I show you?"

He folded his arms across his wide chest and looked at her as if judging her strength. "I need a ring."

She swallowed. "A ring? What kind of ring?"

"A diamond engagement ring."

His words paralyzed her; even her heart stood still. At that moment, more than any other, Chrystal realized how much she loved Max and what she'd sacrificed by giving him up. Pain flooded her empty heart, filling it like a lake that had been dry for years, and the silence grew in the tiny shop until Chrystal managed to gather her wits and the broken pieces of her heart together. "Of course," she answered, her voice a husky whisper. "They're right over here."

Like a wooden soldier, she marched to the case on her left, vaguely aware of Max following her. Her lungs were so tight she couldn't breathe, and the small amount of air reaching them burned as if the shop were on fire. Their gaze met over the case. "Did you have anything special in mind?"

His black eyes, like twin gun barrels, stared her down. "Which one would you choose?"

His question sliced into her heart with ruthless abandonment, but without a second's hesitation, Chrystal reached into the case and pulled out a ring. Silently, she handed the glittering diamond to him.

Max looked down then back up at Chrystal in amazement. "This is the canary stone that was in your necklace."

"That's right," she said evenly. "I bought it back from Hiram."

"Why did you take it out of the necklace setting?"

She shrugged. How could she tell him that the sight of the gorgeous necklace broke her heart every time she looked in the case, the twinkling diamond reminding her only of the man she'd loved but lost. She'd melted down the gold and used it for the ring he now held. "I thought it best."

The giant, yellow stone winked under the lights of the store as Max twisted the piece of jewelry. For several long moments, he looked at the diamond as if making up his mind. The longer he studied the beautiful ring, the deeper the pain cut into her soul.

Suddenly, he reached across the counter and took her left hand in both of his. Before she could say another word, he slipped the ring on her finger. It nestled there, perfectly, as if she'd made it for herself.

"Will you marry me, Chrystal?"

For several heart beats of silence, Chrystal felt her eyes widen and dart from her hand to Max's face then her heart exploded with joyful suspicion.

"Are, are you serious?" she stuttered.

"I've never been more serious in my whole life, and never been a bigger fool, either, than when I let you walk out of my office. I was angry and hurt, but if I let that stand between us, it would be the biggest mistake of my life." He leaned over the counter, her hand still clutched in his. "Please say 'yes,' Chrystal. I need you. I love you. I want to share the rest of your life."

"You, you're buying this for me?"

He grinned and squeezed her fingers. "I'm not asking anyone else to marry me."

"I . . . I thought . . ."

"I know," he said, his dark eyes begging forgiveness, "and I was cruel, but I didn't know what else to do. I didn't think you'd let me in unless I came on business, and I sure as hell couldn't buy you a diamond somewhere else."

He continued to hold her fingers while he lead her to the break in the counter. When they met at the opening, he pulled her hands against his chest. She could feel the flutter of his heart. "The more I thought about your feelings, the more sense your reaction made. You had no idea that Marion had seen the telegram, and I was the only one you'd told about Neal. I would have jumped to the same conclusion." He tightened his grip on her hand. "I was hurt though, that you thought I'd betray your trust."

"I wasn't fair."

"It doesn't matter. I wasn't, either." His jaw tightened, and he held on to her hands as though he'd never let go. "I love you," he said simply. "Please say yes, Chrystal."

Was there any other answer? She looked into the darkness of his eyes and nodded once. He drew her to him and folded his arms around her, and for a long, slow minute, he held her tight, then his head moved and bent to meet hers. They sealed their silent pledge with a kiss while the bright diamond on her finger sparkled with promise.

CHAPTER ELEVEN

SHARE THE FUN . . .
SHARE YOUR NEW-FOUND TREASURE!!

You don't want to let your new books out of your sight? That's okay. Your friends can get their own. Order below.

No. 45 PERSONAL BEST by Margaret Watson
Nick is a cynic; Tess, an optimist. Where does love fit in?

No. 46 ONE ON ONE by JoAnn Barbour
Vincent's no saint but Loie's attracted to the devil in him anyway.

No. 47 STERLING'S REASONS by Joey Light
Joe is running from his conscience; Sterling helps him find peace.

No. 48 SNOW SOUNDS by Heather Williams
In the quiet of the mountain, Tanner and Melaine find each other again.

No. 49 SUNLIGHT ON SHADOWS by Lacey Dancer
Matt and Miranda bring out the sunlight in each other's lives.

No. 50 RENEGADE TEXAN by Becky Barker
Rane lives only for himself—that is, until he meets Tamara.

No. 51 RISKY BUSINESS by Jane Kidwell
Blair goes undercover but finds more than she bargained for with Logan.

No. 52 CAROLINA COMPROMISE by Nancy Knight
Richard falls for Dee and the glorious Old South. Can he have both?

No. 53 GOLDEN GAMBLE by Patrice Lindsey
The stakes are high! Who has the winning hand—Jessie or Bart?

No. 54 DAYDREAMS by Marina Palmieri
Kathy's life is far from a fairy tale. Is Jake her Prince Charming?

No. 55 A FOREVER MAN by Sally Falcon
Max is trouble and Sandi wants no part of him. She *must* resist!

No. 56 A QUESTION OF VIRTUE by Carolyn Davidson
Neither Sara nor Cal can ignore their almost magical attraction.

No. 57 BACK IN HIS ARMS by Becky Barker
Fate takes over when Tara shows up on Rand's doorstep again.

No. 58 SWEET SEDUCTION by Allie Jordan
Libby wages war on Will—she'll win his love yet!

No. 59 13 DAYS OF LUCK by Lacey Dancer
Author Pippa Weldon finds her real-life hero in Joshua Luck.

No. 60 SARA'S ANGEL by Sharon Sala
Sara *must* get to Hawk. He's the only one who can help.

No. 61 HOME FIELD ADVANTAGE by Janice Bartlett
Marian shows John there is more to life than just professional sports.

No. 62 FOR SERVICES RENDERED by Ann Patrick
Nick's life is in perfect order until he meets Claire!

No. 63 WHERE THERE'S A WILL by Leanne Banks
Chelsea goes toe-to-toe with her new, unhappy business partner.

No. 64 YESTERDAY'S FANTASY by Pamela Macaluso
Melissa always had a crush on Morgan. Maybe dreams do come true!

No. 65 TO CATCH A LORELEI by Phyllis Houseman
Lorelei sets a trap for Daniel but gets caught in it herself.

No. 66 BACK OF BEYOND by Shirley Faye
Dani and Jesse are forced to face their true feelings for each other.

No. 67 CRYSTAL CLEAR by Cay David
Max could be the end of all Chrystal's dreams . . . or just the beginning!

No. 68 PROMISE OF PARADISE by Karen Lawton Barrett
Gabriel is surprised to find that Eden's beauty is not just skin deep.
